# INN THE SPIRIT OF COMPETITION

## SPIRITS OF TEXAS
## COZY MYSTERIES, BOOK 3

# BECKI WILLIS

Becki Willis/Clear Creek Publishers
4253 CR 427
Marquez, Texas/ 77865
www.beckiwillis.com

Publisher's Note: This is a work of fiction. Names, characters, places, and incidents are a product of the author's imagination. Locales and public names are sometimes used for atmospheric purposes. Any resemblance to actual people, living or dead, or to businesses, companies, events, institutions, or locales is completely coincidental.

Book Layout © 2017 BookDesignTemplates.com

Inn the Spirit of Trickery/ Becki Willis -- 1st ed.
ISBN  978-1-947686-09-0

# Books by Becki Willis

Forgotten Boxes

Plain Roots

Tangible Spirits

He Kills Me, He Kills Me Not

*Mirrors Don't Lie Series:*

    The Girl from Her Mirror – Book 1

    Mirror, Mirror on Her Wall – Book 2

    Light from Her Mirror – Book 3

*The Sisters, Texas Mystery Series:*

    Chicken Scratch – Book 1

    When the Stars Fall – Book 2

    Stipulations & Complications – Book 3

    Home Again: Starting Over – Book 4

    Genny's Ballad – Book 5

    Christmas In The Sisters – Book 6

    The Lilac Code – Book 7

    Wildflower Wedding – Book 8

    Sitting on a Fortune – Book 9

*Spirits of Texas Cozy Mystery Series:*

    Inn the Spirit of Legends – Book 1

    Inn the Spirit of Trickery – Book 2

*Texas General Cozy Cases:*

    A Case of Murder by Monte Carlo

    A Hand-Me-Down Heart

# CONTENTS

CHAPTER 1 ................................................................. 1

CHAPTER 2 ................................................................. 4

CHAPTER 3 ................................................................. 12

CHAPTER 4 ................................................................. 20

CHAPTER 5 ................................................................. 33

CHAPTER 6 ................................................................. 40

CHAPTER 7 ................................................................. 48

CHAPTER 8 ................................................................. 57

CHAPTER 9 ................................................................. 65

CHAPTER 10 ............................................................... 72

CHAPTER 11 ............................................................... 79

CHAPTER 12 ............................................................... 81

CHAPTER 13 ............................................................... 91

CHAPTER 14 ............................................................... 103

CHAPTER 15 ............................................................... 110

CHAPTER 16 ............................................................... 123

CHAPTER 17 ............................................................... 133

CHAPTER 18 ............................................................... 144

CHAPTER 19 ............................................................... 149

CHAPTER 20 ............................................................... 161

CHAPTER 21 ............................................................... 173

CHAPTER 22 ............................................................... 186

From the Author ...................................................... 193

# CHAPTER 1

"This could be it, Tallia, baby!" The man's voice spiked with excitement. "This could be the big break I've been waiting for."

"You've said that before." On the other end of the line, Tallia's voice sounded bored. She went so far as to yawn.

Lounging poolside at the campground's small aquatic offering, she positioned her legs on the chaise for optimum exposure. Whether that exposure was to the sunshine or to the eye of the opposite sex was debatable.

"But there's a contract with this one," he said. "A big one. The winner of this tournament will be the official spokesman for *Luckenbach Poles*." He paused, waiting for a response that never came.

It was time to bring out the big guns. "There will be commercials that air on national television."

At this, Tallia perked up, just as he had known she would. "TV?" she quizzed. She swung her long legs to a sitting position, all but leaping onto her feet. "I've always wanted to be on TV!"

"Once I get in good with the top brass, I'll tell them I want you in the commercials with me," he promised.

A pout moved into her voice. "How long will that take?"

"I don't know, exactly. I can't just go in making demands. I'll have to ease my way in, you see. I'll need to make a good impression. Get in their good graces, so to say." Before she could sputter out a protest, he hurried on. "I'll have to go in first and get people used to hearing my name, seeing my face. That's when we'll bring you in. With my face and your body, we'll become the people behind the pole. The first thing folks think of when they hear the words *Luckenbach Poles*."

"What's wrong with *my* face?" Tallia demanded. She came fully to her feet, tossing a look at her reflection in the pool. Ripples eddied near the edge, shortening the pull of her elongated face. Wavy lines softened the sharp thrust of her teeth. Even the nicotine stains could be attributed to the dirty tiles below. Tallia presented a wide, toothy smile into the water, pleased with the flattering image it threw back at her, distorted or not.

On the other end of the line, the man grappled for words. He often fantasized about Tallia, but it wasn't her face that kept him awake at night. She had far more attractive assets that held his attention. He was quick to change the subject. "Did I mention the cash prize?"

"Last time," she complained, "you hardly got enough to pay for a cheap hotel."

"Not this time, Tallia baby. This time, the prize is ten grand."

Greed did unkind things to Tallia's already homely face, especially when the ripple in the water widened, carrying the tip of her chin with it. "Ten thousand dollars?" she squeaked in surprise. "*Plus* a TV contract?"

2

"I've waited a long time for this, baby," the man told her. "The time is right. I'm looking good in the standings, and I've got a good feeling about the Hannah Trifishlon. My time has come."

"*Our* time has come," Tallia reminded him. He wasn't going to the top without her. She'd latch onto his coattail with both hands if she had to.

The man made a bold prediction. "It's do or die, Tallia baby. Do or die."

# CHAPTER 2

The man meandered into the sporting goods store, careful to avert his face from the overhead camera. A glance to check the bottom of his boots. A sudden interest in an item to his right. An adjustment of his cap. That's all it took to block a clear view of his face, should the need to review the film ever arise. He kept his movements smooth and unhurried as he casually moved past the electronic eye into the interior of the store.

After three days of studying the shop from the inside out, he knew what to expect. It was early afternoon, when the staff took an informal lunch break. Being a mom and pop business with only a handful of employees, they tended to gather in the breakroom for a communal meal and a discussion of the day's performance thus far. If anything needed mailing or taken to the bank, the Mrs. scuttled out the door while the others lingered over dessert or another glass of iced tea.

He knew that the girl was usually the first to finish and the first to grow bored, there at the table with her parents and her two co-workers. Given the choice between waiting on a customer or sitting at the table, buried in her cell phone or in the wild fish tales being told, she chose the customer every time. She would be up and out of the breakroom before the men could push back their chairs.

She was pretty, too, in a girlish kind of way. Her body was trim and lithe, with a small, firm bust and long, skinny legs that reminded him of a young colt. He judged her to be at the cusp of womanhood, probably fresh out of high school and ready to tackle the world. She had outgrown the gawkiness of her early teens; hadn't yet grown into the confidence and ease of her twenties. Her clothes were just suggestive enough to raise an eyebrow, but modest enough to meet her parents' scrutiny. If he had the time, or the inclination, he might be tempted by her budding beauty, but he had neither.

He preferred women. Women like Tallia, with their fully developed bodies and their years of experience. Their outfits never sent mixed messages. Women like Tallia knew what they wanted, and they made sure everyone else knew it, too. They knew exactly how to dress to catch a man's attention. Best of all, they knew how to act, and what to do, to keep that attention.

The girl called out a greeting long before she reached him. By the time her coltish legs delivered her to his side, she had welcomed him to the store, introduced herself, and asked if she could help him.

He studied her from behind his mirrored aviator glasses, knowing women hated that sort of thing. Deep down, he suspected, it was a love/hate situation, because they never knew exactly where the man's eyes were. Depending on the man, that could be creepy, or it could be exhilarating.

He took his time in answering, allowing his eyes to trail over her so she could feel his gaze, even if she couldn't see it. He let the slightest of smiles curve his lips.

"Well, now, Danika, you may just be able to help me, after all. I'd like to know about fishing in these parts."

"Well, then, you came to just the right place!" she told him with a saucy smile. One toss of her hair said that she didn't put him in the creepy department, even though he was far too old for her.

Little girls and their rush to grow up, he thought with a sigh. If only they could realize this was the best time of their lives, when everything was still new and un-tainted, and anything was still possible.

"Where's the best place to fish?" he asked.

"Depends on what you're fishing for," she shot back.

"Anything."

"Then anywhere."

She knew he was testing her. As a young girl working in a sporting goods store, she had no doubt seen it often enough. It would probably be the same for a man working in a dress shop. No woman would dare trust his judgment until she had tested what he did or didn't know about fashion.

It was the same here in the sporting goods store. He asked enough vague and specific questions to get a feel for her knowledge about fishing. Surprisingly enough, the girl kept up and answered correctly, every single time. They spent the next ten minutes in a fast-paced, witty exchange. He found her a worthy opponent and quite possibly the secret weapon he had hoped for.

He knew that the store was a sponsor for the Trifishlon Tournament, but she didn't know that he knew. He told her he was from far West Texas, where fishing holes were few and far between. He was here on vacation and intended to spend his time pond-hopping, lake-hopping, or river-hopping, whatever the case might be.

Where the fish called, he would answer. Seven glorious days of nothing but him and a hook in the water.

He obtained his first clue quite by accident. When the owner eventually drifted from the back room, a stain of barbecue sauce still fragrant upon his shirt collar, Danika called over her shoulder, "Hey, Dad. If this guy wanted to go to Pedernales Falls State Park to fish, which day would you suggest? Monday or Tuesday?" She used the proper pronunciation of the name, Per-der-na-les.

It would seem a strange question, given the forecast was the same for the foreseeable future. Hot, dry, and sunny, with no chance of rain. Weekday crowds were unpredictable. But if a certain contest happened to be taking place, a contest he supposedly knew nothing about, then the day he visited could make all the difference. He feigned ignorance as he watched her father dart a nervous glance around the room, as if searching for spies.

Cautious, the girl's father came forward to size up the newcomer. "I don't believe we've met. Lou Matejka."

"Joe Don Ellis," he replied smoothly, pulling the alias from thin air. "Your associate has been a great source of information. She's a very knowledgeable woman." He deliberately omitted 'young,' knowing it would gain him favor in her eyes. Not that they weren't already glowing with stars, but every little bit helped.

"Here for the tournament, are you?" the owner asked.

He scrunched his face with just the right amount of confusion. "Tournament? I don't know anything about a tournament. I'm just here for a week of fishing. Just me, a cold six pack, and a wet hook in the water." He rocked back on his heels, looking the part of a dreamy fisherman. He allowed the moment to linger, as he presumably marveled over his dumb luck to be granted such a week. Then he shifted, as if a thought suddenly occurred to him. "Oh,

7

hey. Wait. What kind of tournament? Is it too late to get in on it? I might be interested."

"Sorry. Registration's already ended."

"Oh, well. Easy come, easy go." He spread his hands in a carefree fashion. "Not sure that fits into my plans for the week, anyway. I don't plan to get in any hurry."

They chatted for a moment, and he pretended interest in a few maps the owner suggested. He asked enough innocent questions about the area to sound like a total novice. By the time the owner thanked him for coming in and drifted back to more important tasks, he felt sure his cover was safe.

At the last minute, Lou Matejka turned back and offered, "Oh, and if I were you, I'd visit Pedernales Falls on Tuesday."

"Good to know. Appreciate the tip, man." He grinned. It may or may not mean anything, but it was a start. He turned to the girl still by his side and winked. Even though she couldn't see his eyes behind the glasses, something in her demeanor said she picked up on it, anyway.

"That tournament sounds kind of interesting," he said. "Can anyone watch?"

"I, uh, I'm not sure. I'm not at liberty to give out any information."

"Ah, I get it. They don't let you in on things, huh?" There was a hint of sympathy in his voice. Just the right amount of pacified coddling to suggest she was too young or too insignificant to be kept in the loop.

The girl bristled, as he hoped she would. "It's not that," she said in a stiff voice.

"Hey, I get it. They never let us peons in on the big stuff. Same with my boss. It's like they think we can't be trusted with important details. Don't sweat it." He lifted his shoulder to suggest it didn't matter.

Turned away to inspect a nearby jacket, as if she didn't matter.

After a slight hesitation, the girl took the bait. She stepped closer, so that the words she spoke didn't carry. "Actually, we're sponsoring the tournament, so I know all about it. I'm just not at liberty to divulge any of the details."

"Hey, I get it." He held up both palms in acceptance, but he sounded less than convincing.

"You don't believe me," Danika accused. She crossed her arms beneath her small breasts in challenge.

"Sure, I do," he patronized her.

The girl looked over her shoulder, making certain her father and co-workers were otherwise engaged. "It's just that they've upped the prize money this year, so they're keeping everything all hush-hush."

He heard the defensive tone in her voice, and he knew he had her exactly where he wanted her.

"You're cute when you get all riled up," he drawled. He let his eyes walk over her again. He traced his bottom lip with the tip of his tongue, chuckling softly when he saw her flush with pleasure.

"I'm not riled up," she lied. "I just don't like it when someone doesn't believe me."

"I said I believed you."

She rolled her eyes in true teenage fashion. "You're a terrible liar."

He bit the inside of his mouth so that only a sheepish smile leaked out. If only you knew! He kept the thought to himself. He tried to sound apologetic as he supposedly 'admitted' to the claim. "Yeah, that's what my ex always said."

Responding to his reference of being single, the girl dropped her arms. Feigning distraction, she fingered the jacket he inspected. "It's just that they keep certain elements of the contest secret until the last minute," she volunteered. "So even if I wanted to, I can't tell any of the details."

The slight inflection of the word tell was an invitation in itself. Trying not to gloat, he ran his hand over the front of the jacket, fake testing the hang of the fabric. When his fingers brushed against hers, she didn't pull away, telling him everything he needed to know.

"Hey." He used an intimate tone, puckering his forehead to convince her of his sincerity. "I understand. I respect your vow to secrecy. The last thing I want to do is cause a pretty lady like you any trouble. I'm just passing through, looking for a week of fun in the sun, and... whatever distractions may come my way." He swayed ever so slightly inward as he added the last, laughing when her cheeks pinked.

He pretended to take mercy on her. He kept his tone light. Flirty. "So tell me, pretty lady. Highly classified secrets aside, if a fella wanted to fish like he was in this tournament, which pole would you recommend?" He walked backwards, until he reached the first display of fishing poles. She followed like an eager puppy.

He pulled out a kid's Spiderman pole. "Is this what I'd need?"

She giggled at his antics and rolled her eyes. "Hardly."

"What about this?" He moved to a seven-foot fiberglass rod.

She pursed her lips, pretending to give his suggestion thought. "Close, but no cigar."

He reached for a more sophisticated, higher-priced rod. One that bore their own brand's logo. "What about this one?"

"That one may be out of your price range," she warned, her eyes twinkling.

He pulled his wallet from his shorts pocket and pulled out three crisp, one-hundred-dollar bills. "I have a generous budget for the week," he told her. This time, there was nothing playful about his tone.

"In that case..." With a shrewd smirk on her face, the girl stretched past him, allowing her body to brush against his. "I might suggest this one. If you were fishing with the big guys. If you were asking, and if I could say." She pulled a fly-fishing pole from the rack, knowing it was the deluxe model. Despite its state-of-the-art design, few fishermen were prepared to pay for such precision craftsmanship.

This might be her parents' business, but she still worked on commission.

# CHAPTER 3

"I still don't know why I let you and Fred talk me into this," Hannah Duncan moaned, not for the first time. Nerves pooled in her stomach and made it ache. A vague headache hummed behind her eyelids, threatening to pick up momentum at any minute. The faster her heart galloped in her chest, the more focused the headache became.

"That's just your nerves talking," Sadie Turner assured her. "This place is hopping, girl. This is a record turnout for the qualifying round. Our best start ever for the Trifishlon! Just look at that crowd out there."

Hannah's reply, dry as sawdust, lacked the older woman's enthusiasm. "I see that crowd. Why do you think I'm so nervous?"

For Sadie, hosting the fishing tournament was old hat. Having helped create the annual competition, she had had her hand in the event for each of its twenty-three years of existence. She had long since forgotten the nerve-racking anticipation of a first-time host.

But for Hannah, this was the first time. She was still new to the whole innkeeper thing, without the added drama of hosting a fishing tournament. Four months in, she was still dealing with the enormity of not only running the historic inn, but of owning it.

Today's event was the kickoff to the annual fishing tournament, cranked up to new heights.

A few weeks ago, Hannah had innocently mentioned "what if." The next thing she knew, Sadie and Fred had taken her ideas and ran with them. More than simply another 'first' for the novice innkeeper, today was the day of reckoning for her newly implemented ideas.

"There's nothing to be nervous about, girl," Sadie insisted. "Clearly, your ideas were exactly what this tired old event needed! Fresh blood is always a good thing, 'specially for us old timers who are set in our ways and too stiff to bend. Adding a junior fishing contest was genius. Half of those people yonder are kids, and anytime you can get kiddos away from their gadgets and out in the fresh air, involved in nature, it's a sure winner. Finding new sponsors and upping the ante was a stroke of brilliance, too. So stop fretting. Those wrinkles will set in your face and make you look old beyond your years."

If Hannah had learned one thing from her absentee mother, it was the importance of youthful-looking skin. Jacqueline Duncan, former daytime soap queen and commercial countess wannabe, instilled the importance of good skin care in her only daughter. It was one of the few valuable pieces of advice Jacqueline had given her.

Schooling the frown from her face, Hannah attempted a tight smile. "Is this better?"

With a gruff snort, her friend muttered, "As long as no little children see you. Otherwise, it will scare a year's growth out of them." Sadie jabbed a fleshy elbow into Hannah's side and sat up straighter in her lawn chair. "Okay, here comes the biggest test of all. Bart Hinkle."

It was the way she said the man's name, as if she couldn't get the bitter taste from her mouth quick enough. Hannah knew he was trouble, even before she looked up and saw his scowl.

"Sadie Tanner!" he boomed, long before he reached a conversational distance. "What is the meaning of this highway robbery? Have you plumb lost your mind, woman?"

"Last time I checked," she shot back smartly, "it was still where I left it, Bart Hinkle." She tapped the top of her gray curls for visual confirmation.

The fisherman huffed and puffed the last few feet to the table, rocking his bulky form across the uneven terrain. He wore overalls, Army boots, and a cap that sat slightly off-kilter atop his receding hairline. Jabbing a thick finger, he pointed to the tabletop sign. "I've been coming to this tournament for twelve or more years! I've never paid that sort of price a single time!"

A long folding table sat beneath the sheltering arms of an ancient live oak, protecting the women from the sun. Numbered paper bags, sealed and lined up in neat rows, sat to the side of two large signs. One listed the rules for the tournament. The other, the one Bart Hinkle stabbed with his accusatory glare, stated the entry fee.

"Two hundred dollars!" he bellowed. "Two hundred dollars! That's highway robbery! Over twice the normal $75 fee."

"I'm pleased to see you've been brushing up on your math skills, Bart," Sadie all but snickered. She turned to the woman at her side with a proud smile. "Bart, I don't believe you've had the pleasure of meeting our new owner, Hannah Duncan. Hannah, this blowhard is Bart Hinkle, from down Galveston way. Don't let his gruff manner insult you. It's just his way."

Despite his ire, Bart Hinkle knew the proper way to greet a lady. He doffed his cap and offered a quick nod to the young beauty at Sadie's side. "Pleasure to meet you, ma'am. Any relation to Miss Wilhelmina?"

In a strange twist of fate—and aided by her wealthy uncle's interference— Hannah didn't just own The Spirits of Texas Inn; she owned the entire town in which it sat. Hannah, Texas consisted of the old stage-coach stop, a handful of original buildings, a hodgepodge

14

of farm animals, frontage to South Grape Creek, and the sparkling body of water currently edged with anglers of all ages. As the last descendant of the founding family, Wilhelmina Hannah owned the town until her death a few months ago. She was also the creator of the Trifish-lon.

Extending her arm for a handshake, Hannah offered a polite smile. "Hello, Mr. Hinkle. No, I'm afraid all we shared was a name. Mine as a first, hers as a last. But I'm trying to live up to the expectations she left behind, even though sometimes that means changing things a bit. I think you'll find the extra entry fee is money well spent."

He had the grace to look sorry for his outburst, but he couldn't resist a lingering whine. "But to go from seventy-five to two hundred..."

"Twenty-five of that will go to fight hunger, right here in our community," Hannah proudly informed him. "And I'm sure you noticed that we've upped the prize this year for the winner. In the past, only one person received a prize, which was one thousand dollars and a big cooler full of beer and fishing lures. This year, that's the second-place prize. First place is ten thousand dollars, plus national recognition as Luckenbach Poles official spokesperson." Even if the overall effort was a fail, Hannah was proud to have secured a generous sponsor in Luckenbach Poles.

She cocked her dark head to the side and put meaning into her smile. "I think the extra hundred dollars is certainly worth the chance to win it, don't you?"

"In case you didn't practice your multiplication tables," Sadie offered in an overly sweet voice, "that would be a ten-time return on that extra hundred dollars."

"I know what it is!" the fisherman snapped. He pulled out a hundred-dollar bill and a paper sack. The bag made an odd clinking sound as he smacked it onto the table. "Here's my entry fee. I'd like twenty-one, seeing as it's my lucky number."

Daring the wrinkles of time, Hannah frowned again. "Twenty-one?" she questioned in confusion.

"Yeah, I want number twenty-one. I'm always twenty-one," Bart insisted.

"You're three times that, if you're a day!" Sadie muttered under her breath, causing Hannah to bite back a smile.

"I'm afraid it doesn't work like that, Mr. Hinkle," she explained. "We're handing out numbers chronologically. You're the thirteenth angler to check in, so you're number thirteen."

"Oh, hell no, I ain't!" the man complained, taking a step backward. "You can't make me be unlucky thirteen! I'll take twenty-one, same as I always do."

Determined to stand her ground, Hannah's smile never wavered. "In that case, please step aside and wait until that number is available."

"And let someone else get the jump on me? There's already twelve people before me! I'm not about to sit out and let another half dozen get their spot before I do!" he bellowed.

He should have polished his math skills a bit more, Hannah mused silently. Aloud, she spoke in a smooth, no-nonsense voice. "Very well. Number thirteen it is."

"No! I refuse to take it."

Behind him, another man spoke. "I'll take it. I'm not afraid of some silly superstition."

Hannah's smile was genuine as she turned her attention to the newcomer. "Thank you very much, sir. I will be happy to check you in as the official Number 13. Your name?"

"Rand Galloway."

"What do you mean, Galloway?" Bart snarled. "Can't you wait your turn like the rest? Or do you think being a three-time winner makes you better than the rest of us?"

"I'm just trying to get checked in, Hinkle, same as you. But unlike you, I don't think my winning hinges on a number. I rely on skill for that." He pulled two crisp

16

hundred-dollar bills from his pocket and handed them to Hannah with a charming wink. "Where do I sign, madam?"

"Right here. Sadie will give you your number and your bag with the lures needed for today's qualification round."

Bart Hinkle continued to sputter objections while the other man shamelessly flirted with Hannah. As Rand Galloway moved along down the table to cast his charms upon Sadie, Bart thrust his hand forward. "Fine. I'll take fourteen."

"I'm assuming the rest of your fee is in the bag?" Hannah asked, eying the bulging bottom of the small paper sack.

"That's right. I had to rob my piggy bank to pay the exorbitant entry free." He was no longer apologetic about his complaints. He was outright obnoxious, smirking as he nodded to the bag in question. "Go ahead, count it. It's all there. One hundred dollars. In change." He darted a worried look to Rand Galloway's retreating back, knowing the other angler was getting the jump on him. Wiggling his fingers with impatience, he barked, "Hurry up! Give me my number."

"Oh, I have to count it first, sir, and confirm the correct entry fee." Hannah never batted an eye as she put the rude man in his place. "There's a line forming behind you, so please step aside until we're able to count your change. With any luck, you may be able to get your favorite number, after all."

"What? What!" He worked himself into a rage, his face turning the color of an overripe eggplant. "You can't just—"

Before he could finish his sentence, wind rustled through the leaves of the mighty oak. The gust didn't seem that strong, but a wayward branch mysteriously dipped and smacked the angler in the face, knocking his cap from his head. A second breeze carried it a few feet away from the table. Bart hurried after it, but as he bent to retrieve his hat, the clasp on his overalls came undone, and the strap slipped from his shoulder. With a bit of a

17

squeal, the big man ducked behind the tree and saved his audience from a ghastly sight.

Laughing, Hannah knew she had her friend Orlan Valera to thank. People who thought ghosts were scary obviously didn't know the spirits haunting her property. Ghost or not, the faithful vaquero had been nothing but helpful. In fact, he had saved her life on two separate occasions. Even Gouyen, the stoic Native American medicine woman, had proved helpful, if not friendly. And Caroline... well, the poor Southern belle wasn't right in the head, but she was hardly a threat. Hannah was proud to consider all three apparitions as friends.

She caught a glimpse of Orlan's wispy form swirling upward through the treetop as she called out, "Next?"

A woman stepped up, shepherding two children in front of her. "I'd like to enter these two in the Junior Fish-Off."

"Absolutely! That will be fifty dollars, please. And I'll need you to fill out this form."

Once the three moved down the table toward Sadie, another woman stepped up in their place. "Hello. I need to check in and pay for the tournament. You should have the paperwork for Sly Patterson."

Hannah checked her pre-populated list for the name. "Yes, I've got the information right here." She looked beyond the sandy-haired woman for a companion. "Is Sly with you?"

"I'm Sly," the woman informed her, looking only slightly irritated at the blunder that, no doubt, happened all too often.

"Oh, I'm so sorry," Hannah gushed.

She waved the apology aside. "No worries. The very first tournament I entered, they misspelled Syl, short for Sylvia, as Sly. The name just sort of stuck after that."

"Well, Sly, welcome to the qualifying round for the Hannah Trifishlon. I see this is your first time here, so are you clear about today's rules?"

"Closed-faced reels only, twenty-pound line max. Use only the lures and bait supplied in the bag you provide. Bags and contents are selected randomly, no preference given. There are three weigh-in times throughout the afternoon. All fish are fair fish, total weight wins. Top twelve go on to compete in the Trifishlon." Sylvia Patterson rambled through the rules as if she read them from a script. When finished, she flashed a smile that softened her ordinary, makeup-free face and gave it the adornment needed to be considered pretty. "Did I forget anything?"

"Just that you have the option to catch and release, or catch and donate. The fish fry starts at dusk. Plates are $10, and all proceeds will be donated to the local food pantry, along with a portion of each tournament entry fee."

Sly dipped her a sandy-blond ponytail in a quick nod. "Got it."

"Perfect. You can collect your number and bag with Sadie. Please pin the number to the back of your shirt so that it's visible at all times. Again, welcome to Hannah."

Two more people went through the line before Hannah had an opportunity to count coins from Bart Hinkle's rumpled sack. She was interrupted twice, one of which times she had to start her counting over. By the time the man was finally given his number (Number 19), he was quietly fuming, but there were no more outbursts from him.

Not until he lost out to a woman.

# CHAPTER 4

The goal of the Hannah Trifishlon was to master the fine art of fishing. Each phase of the tournament was designed to explore a different aspect and a different approach to the sport. Rather than relying on fancy riggings and specialized equipment, anglers were encouraged to depend on natural talent and adapting to one's surroundings.

To that end, the specifics of each round were highly confidential. Styles and locations were kept secret until the last moment. Contest rules required that anglers use only the bait, lures, and gear given to them by the venue. For the qualifying round, the selections were varied and totally random, adding to the challenge.

As always, there were a few who grumbled about the bait bag they received. There was inevitably some disgruntled angler claiming they had drawn the short end of the stick, putting them at a disadvantage against their more fortunate peers. Hannah expected to hear as much from Bart Hinkle, but the man never made a peep about his assigned gear.

The afternoon passed swiftly, broken in part by three official weigh-ins. Fish were hauled to the scales, weighed, and dutifully recorded in the official logbook. Fred Tanner wrote the top three weights on a huge chalkboard, omitting the names of the anglers. A smaller board was kept, every bit as diligently, for the junior fisherman of the day. Prizes for those winners would be awarded before the top anglers were announced at dusk.

A diverse group of local leaders served as judges. Life-long resident and local attorney Walker Jacoby. Four-term county judge Robert Lee McNutt. 4-H Leader and County Fair coordinator Melinda Benswanger. Local businessman and Chamber of Commerce president Alonzo vanCleef.

Even so, when disqualified for using his own lure, one of the contestants cried foul. He cited prejudice against him, although he failed to say which judge was at fault.

Two other contestants were disqualified for fighting. The men were known rivals and recently had a similar run-in at another tournament on Lake LBJ. Although alcohol was clearly prohibited during the qualification round, they had each smuggled in a flask and helped themselves to the banned refreshment. Between the dual violations of drinking and fighting, both men were asked to leave the premises.

It was no wonder emotions ran high. The contestants were vying for twelve coveted spots, plus one official alternate.

The Texas sun had been relentless, refusing to hide behind clouds on that blistering day. By the time dusk arrived, ushered in on a much-welcomed breeze, tempers flared, and trash talk flew. Before winners could be announced, another small skirmish had broken out, and Walker Jacoby threatened to disqualify them if they couldn't be cordial.

21

After a long verification process by all four judges, Hannah took the makeshift stage for the required speeches, sponsor recognition, thank yous, and such. Over the grumbling voices of a few impatient fishermen, they announced the junior tournament winners first. Each child won a small prize and had their picture taken by the local paper and beaming parents.

The tantalizing smell of fried fish and hush puppies filled the air as the crowd pushed in closer to hear the names of the twelve finalists. While the general population drifted away in favor of food, the pro and semi-pro anglers waited in hopes of hearing their name called.

Making the announcements, Fred Tanner was a born entertainer and knew how to captivate a crowd. The petite woman was no longer a sweetheart of the rodeo, dazzling people with her trick riding and equine skills, but she was still a performer. She offered witty anecdotes and special memories of years past as she built up to the final twelve reveal. It was her equivalent to a drum roll.

Just before people became restless, she called the first name. It was no surprise that Rand Galloway had the heaviest bag and made first finalist. Three other shoo-ins followed, trailed by a couple of surprise winners. As the number of entry spots dwindled, fishermen shifted on their feet, anxious and uncertain.

"And the last finalist, clenching the number twelve spot in this year's Trifishlon tournament," Fred called, her voice strong and clear in the hushed evening air, "is none other than our very first female contestant, Sly Patterson!"

As applause broke out and Sly squealed in delight, Bart Hinkle made his protests clear. "Now see here! I don't think a female is qualified in this here contest! I think it's against the rules."

"What?" Sly whirled around in outrage, her eyes snapping with anger. "How dare you make such an outrageous claim! You're just prejudiced."

"I like women just fine," the hefty man argued. "As long as they know their place and don't butt in where they don't belong."

There were murmurs of protest throughout the crowd, half of them coming from men. It was Fredrika Tanner who spoke up the loudest, aided as she was by the mic.

"Now see here, Bart Hinkle. This very contest was created by women. You know good and well that Wilhelmina Hannah, Sadie, and I started this tournament over twenty years ago. You never seemed to have a problem with females being in a prominent position during that time. Especially not the two years you won! Willie would be tickled to death that we have our first female angler participating in the tournament, and I'll not abide another cross word on the subject coming out of your sorry mouth."

"Yeah, Hinkle," Rand Galloway pitched in. "If you had a problem with any of the contestants, you should have addressed the matter with the judges before the contest started, not waiting until you were bested to stir up trouble. Take it like a man and admit that Sly won, fair and square."

"Fair?" Bart roared. "There wasn't anything fair about it! She used her womanly wiles to make the cut."

"She used her womanly wise, as in wisdom, to make finalist, Bart Hinkle," Fred insisted. She knew all about the challenges of being a female in a predominately male sport. She secretly hoped the woman would take home the grand prize, tipping the scales for equality ever closer to something that resembled balance.

"She used something, all right." The man didn't know when to shut up. "I want to see her bag! I want those fish cut open! How do we know she didn't soak down one of those feminine napkins and stuff it in the mouth of a catfish, adding to its weight?"

23

All four judges stood at once, speaking over the other. "You're not only out of line, you're out of here!" collided with "I demand you apologize and remove yourself from the contest!"' Two other "Disqualified!" rulings rang amid them.

"You heard the judges," Fred announced. "Bart Hinkle, you are disqualified from the tournament. And it's a shame, because you would have been named as first alternate. As it is, we'll need to name another. Judges, could you please supply us with a more qualified alternate, someone who knows how to abide by the code of conduct befitting a true sportsman?"

After a quick consultation, the judges named Gil Mendoza as the official alternate.

Bart Hinkle continued an angry sputter in the background. He complained about the treatment he had received since checking in that morning, citing the new rules and the outrageous price gouging. He even took exception with Rand's stepping in to take the unlucky Number 13, saying that by doing so, he had somehow transferred the hex to him, since the number should have been his. No one listened to his rant, and soon he sauntered away to sulk in his own misery.

"I'm just glad he's gone," Hannah said as they gathered up loose paraphernalia. "Good riddance."

"Oh, he's not gone," Sadie informed her. "He checked in this afternoon. He's booked into the RV park, same as every year."

"Why would he stay, if he's disqualified?" Baffled, Hannah wanted to know.

Fred had the answer. "First off, he's probably taken vacation and already planned a week's visit. He's paid his rental space and hauled that monstrosity of a motor home up from the coast. And he can still watch the tournament, even if he's not part of it. A lot of folks do."

"And if I know Bart—" Sadie said.

"—which, unfortunately, we do—" her sister pitched in, as they both did when the other was speaking. More often than not, they finished the other's sentence.

"—he'll stick around just to keep trouble stirred up. He'll watch everything like a hawk and shriek twice as loud when he sees something he feels is questionable."

"That includes your relationship with Walker," Fred reluctantly added, dropping her voice an octave. "I hate to say this, but you two better cool things down while this tournament is going on. We can't have even a hint of controversy surrounding the judges or the disqualification process."

"If things cool down any more than they already have," Hannah all but sulked, "they'll freeze over. Between his workload, the summer tourist season, and now this tournament, we've barely seen each other! We've had a grand total of one date, and that was cut short when one of his clients called with an emergency."

"I'm not sure that counted as a date, dear," Sadie told her gently. "Sister and I tagged along with you for dinner that night, remember?"

"I was looking on the bright side," Hannah reasoned. "We actually walked into a restaurant together and ate a meal that wasn't here by the pond or at our kitchen table."

Fred gave her arm a comforting pat. "Your time is coming, dear. Just not during this tournament. It will all be over in less than a week and—"

"—you two can concentrate on going out on a genuine date," Sadie finished. She clasped her hands together, her eyes taking on a dreamy glow. "We'll help you fix your hair and get you a manicure, and you can dress up in one of those pretty little sundresses you brought with you but never get to wear. You can go out on the town, just the two of you."

"I'll believe it when it happens," Hannah sighed. "Right now, we need to head over to the fish fry and make certain things are going smoothly there. I don't think I can handle another confrontation this evening."

"Then you may not want to join the fish fry," Fred warned.

Before she could ask why, Sadie volunteered, "We banned alcohol during fishing, but all bets are off for tonight. There's usually more than a fair share of beer and liquor going around. After a stressful day of hard work and heat—"

"—mixed with sore losers and crushed expectations—"

"—it can make for a very messy evening."

"Good to know. But, as the official host for this event, I feel it's my duty to mingle."

"You have a point," the sisters conceded. "We'll be along shortly."

Not for the first time, Hannah muttered unkind things about her uncle as she trudged around to the far side of the pond where the fish fry was currently in full swing. This was all his fault, after all.

Since ghosts are apparently a real thing, she thought, what about hexing? If she concentrated hard enough, maybe she could send a bevy of bees swarming around JoeJoe's laughing face. Call up a plague of locusts to descend upon him. Better yet, she decided with a malicious grin, frogs! She imagined him covered in warts.

Hannah quickly discarded that notion. Knowing her uncle, he would make yet another fortune off frog legs, and the last thing JoeJoe needed was more money. It was that excess of money and his warped sense of gift giving that had landed her here in the first place.

Not many people were presented with a town for their thirtieth birthday, but then again, most people didn't have the overgrown man-child Joseph Duncan for an uncle. As his only niece, Hannah was the recipient of many strange and outrageous gifts. In the overall scope of things, she supposed receiving a town filled with ramshackled buildings and lingering spirits wasn't all that unusual.

It had been one of those online things. A town, offered at auction via the internet, per the wishes conveyed in Wilhelmina Hannah's will. On a whim, JoeJoe put in a bid, thinking it great fun to gift his niece with a town bearing her name. Caught up in the spirit of online bidding, he ultimately paid an exorbitant price for the property, sight unseen. Making matters worse, he neglected to read the fine print. By the time Hannah checked out her gift and discovered it came with ironclad stipulations, her uncle was across the globe in Dubai, attending business matters with his mega-million-dollar oil company.

Caught in an impossible situation—she had recently lost not just her job, but her entire career and possibly her credibility—Hannah grudgingly accepted the gift and its many responsibilities. She had taken on the challenge if for no reason but to prove that the gift, given as a fluke, could actually become her new life calling. The promise of five thousand dollars, awarded upon her first anniversary, didn't hurt, either.

That was before she knew that the property came with another bonus, this one in the shadowy form of three resident ghosts. By the time she discovered them, she was truly stuck.

She still hadn't seen JoeJoe and given him a proper piece of her mind.

Nor had she given him a hug. Whether she wanted to admit it or not, the town of Hannah had been the best present she had ever received.

Not that she was ready to tell her uncle the truth just yet. Let him languish for a while longer, believing he

27

had given her the ultimate gift of whimsy, yet still fearing her wrath. No doubt, it made for a great story at one of his cocktail parties, or while gathered around a high-stakes poker table. "I once gave my niece her very own town, bearing her name, no less!" No need to let him know just yet that it had been a godsend.

Thanks to JoeJoe, she had two new best friends and a man worthy of her heart. The Tanner sisters were almost old enough to be her grandmothers, but the women shared a kindred spirit not defined by age. And Walker... well, it was still too soon to know about Walker, but the man was one fine kisser, and a truly good person. He was as much a part of her success as the maiden sisters were.

The night sky had darkened by the time Hannah reached the far side of the water. Strings of twinkling lights lit the area for safety and a sense of festivity. The entire side of a catering truck unfolded into a portable kitchen, its massive fryers providing the delicious aromas and flavors of the evening meal. Mounds of fish, caught fresh from the water beyond and fried to a golden crisp, accompanied hush puppies, French fries, and a huge vat of pinto beans to serve the hungry crowd. Untold gallons of sweet tea and an array of homemade desserts, most provided by Sadie herself, added the final touch to the feast.

Families gathered around the makeshift tables in the center of the lights. Along the edges were the teenagers, clustered together in giggling groups, held safe within the fringe of light while asserting a stab at independence. The drinkers huddled in the shadows, pulling out their bottles of beer and whiskey, reliving the day's wins and losses, and making wild predictions for the Trifishlon's outcome. Hannah moved among the crowd, murmuring greetings and offering a welcoming smile to those she passed. She filled a plate, but only nibbled at the food.

Exhaustion and the day's heat had robbed her of her appetite.

As she circled back around, intending to speak to the caterer, movement in the shadows caught her eye. She could hear the low, angry tone of voices above the hum of the generators. Hannah eased closer, fearing the argument could escalate into a fight. It was the last thing she wanted to deal with tonight.

She distinguished the shape of three men in the darkness. Two men stood with their backs to her, facing a third. Their voices were sharp and accusing.

"We know how you operate," one man challenged. "We know you play dirty."

A weak twinkle of light fell across the lone man's face. It was just enough for Hannah to identify him as Rand Galloway, the favored winner for the championship. Hannah didn't recognize the other men, but whoever they were, they were angry with Rand.

"I play to win. And I win because I'm the better fisherman. Any day of the week."

"We'll see about that!" one of the men said, jabbing his finger into Rand's chest.

Taken by surprise, the lead fisherman staggered back a step. Three seconds later, he puffed his chest out and bowed up to the other man. Hannah worried a fight would ensue, but Rand growled out something she couldn't hear and abruptly turned and walked away.

The other two men squabbled between themselves for a moment before the shorter one threw his hands up in exasperation and stomped off in the opposite direction.

The man left standing alone didn't stay that way for long. From the shadows, a woman stepped out and wound herself around him. All Hannah knew was that the woman had long legs and wore ridiculously high heels, given the fact they were in a pasture alongside a glorified stock pond. She watched in amazement as those legs, encased in skin-tight leggings, worked their way around the man and climbed up to his waist, locking behind him. Hannah only had a glimpse of the woman's long, homely face before the couple faded into the shadows to find a moment of passion.

Feeling dirty for having witnessed the scene, Hannah turned away and almost collided with Walker Jacoby.

"Walker! You scared me!"

He eyed her suspiciously. "You look like you ate a rotten lemon."

"I just witnessed a little hanky-panky in the shadows. Who's the woman in skintight pants and four-inch stilettos? You know, perfect attire for a pasture party in the heat of July." Her voice dripped with sarcasm, thick as the Texas humidity around them.

Walker gave a knowing nod of his dark and handsome head, his sigh sounding weary. "That would be Tallia Haney. Technically, she's married to one of the finalists, Kent Haney. But I understand theirs is best described as an open marriage, if you know what I mean."

"So, I take it that wasn't Kent she disappeared into the shadows with?" Hannah ventured to guess.

"Guess not. That's him over there, getting another helping of Sadie's peach cobbler." She followed his gaze to a slightly built man in a plaid fishing shirt. Lover Boy had worn a t-shirt.

"Sounds like the fishing circuit can be as sordid as the Wild West show circuit," Hannah murmured. During the grand re-opening of the inn, she had taken JoeJoe's 'Go Big, or Go Home' mantra to heart and hired a Wild West show as bonus entertainment. Given its traveling soap opera-style relationships and a murder, the bonus angle was debatable.

"I guess every claim to fame comes with its own ragtag team of groupies." Walker shrugged.

"Does that extend to lawyers?" she teased. She knew for a fact that the handsome attorney had a string of admirers, herself included.

It was no wonder. At just over six feet tall, he had a trim build with well-defined muscles. Black hair, a perfect aquiline nose, clear blue eyes, and an understated air of confidence made him a very attractive man.

"You tell me," he murmured, eyes lingering on her mouth with quiet hunger.

Hannah sucked in an uneven breath. "The sisters say we need to be careful, lest people get a wrong impression about us."

Walker visibly stiffened, a posture she knew all too well, given their rocky start. For the first several weeks, they fought their attraction to one another, primarily because he felt a relationship with her would be unprofessional. As her attorney and the executor of Wilhelmina Hannah's will, he vainly tried keeping her at arm's distance. Somehow, however, his arms insisted on reaching for her, and a few weeks ago, they had admitted their mutual attraction and given in to a few exploratory kisses. As she told the sisters, their busy schedules hadn't allowed for much more, but it wasn't because she wasn't willing.

"I thought we established the fact that they wouldn't be wrong," he said, his voice stilted. "Have you changed your mind?"

"No!" she said hastily. She even went as far as touching his arm, darting a guilty glance around to see if anyone noticed. "That's not it at all. But with so much going on this summer... and now with you being a tournament judge and me being a sponsor of the contest..."

"I get it. We can't do anything that could be construed as inappropriate."

31

Hannah nodded glumly as she dropped her hand. "Maybe Tallia is on to something, sneaking off in the shadows," she muttered, only half under her breath.

"It might be a little crowded out there, but I share your sentiment," Walker admitted. His voice deepened to a low rumble. "Soon, Hannah. As soon as this tournament is over, I'm taking you on an actual date. As much as I love Sadie and Fred, it's just going to be the two of us next time."

"I plan to hold you to it. And since I see a couple of people looking our way, I'm going to pretend to thank you for all you did today and go on about my way." She extended a stiff hand and took a step backwards, trying for a professional air.

"Absolutely, Miss Duncan. Anytime," Walker boomed in his best lawyer's voice. "I'll be back for the next phase of the contest. Feel free to call my office if I can be of assistance before then."

Hannah nodded with a glib smile, all the while marveling between clenched teeth. "You're really good at this."

His blue eyes took on a sparkle only she could see. Smooth as silk, he sent goosebumps skittering across her skin as he murmured, "You ain't seen nothing yet, Miss Duncan."

# CHAPTER 5

If Hannah thought her day was over when she left the fish fry, she was sadly mistaken. With the final twelve contestants decided, they needed rooms for the night, and rules required that they stay onsite. Fred said it had something to do with assuring the integrity of the contest, but Hannah thought it was merely a smart business move on Wilhelmina's part.

The guidelines strongly urged contestants to book early, as all rooms were first come, first serve. Only rooms with one bed were guaranteed private; all others were subject to shared occupancy. A few of the fishermen, like Bart Hinkle, Rand Galloway, and Davy Mulligan, had the foresight (or was it the confidence?) to book RV pads ahead of time, and Peanut Ayers had reserved a room for himself and his wife weeks ago. Most of the group, however, waited for the cut before committing to a room.

With summer in full swing, and the Texas Hill Country being a popular vacation spot, making room for the participating anglers stretched the complex to its seams. In truth, it didn't take more than three or four dozen guests to fill the Spirits of Texas Inn complex to capacity. A scant six guest rooms nestled within the main inn; four of those were double occupancy only. Three restored cabins, original to the historical settlement, accommodated additional visitors in rustic charm. A few more guests could squeeze in at the five RV pads and two tent-only campsites along the creek, but it made for a packed and busy little town.

Now that she knew Sly Patterson was a woman, Hannah ear-marked a private room for the lone female finalist. That meant she still needed to leave nine beds open.

A crowd gathered at the desk in front of her, clamoring for attention.

"I was here first," one man claimed. "I'd like the blue room, please. Second on the left."

"No, I was here first," the man at his elbow said. "And I'll take any room you have, as long as it has a hot shower and a bed. A shared cabin is fine by me."

"Has my wife been in here yet?" the third man asked, looking around for the missing woman. "Tall and long legged, with frizzy red hair?"

Hannah bit her lip, resisting the urge to suggest he check the darkened shadows beyond the pond.

It took awhile, but Hannah eventually assigned accommodations to all the guests. The only one to grumble was Melvin Maddox, the man requesting the blue room. Other than Bart Hinkle, he was also the only person to complain about the increased entry fee.

Just when she thought the old inn was quiet and settled for the evening, Hannah spotted the hem of a yellow dress near the top of the stairs.

Caroline.

Biting back a groan, Hannah went in search of the wandering spirit. With a little coaxing, perhaps she could entice the apparition to leave their guests in peace for the evening. Not that the prim and proper Southern belle was in the habit of making a scene, but occasionally, a guest had the ability to see ghosts. It rarely ended well.

"Caroline?" Hannah called softly. "Are you up here?"

She tiptoed down the long hallway, trying to be as quiet as possible. When she detected the faint hint of lavender, she knew the spirit was nearby. "Caroline?"

According to legend, Caroline was a victim of the afterlife, caught in a cosmic glitch that prevented her from crossing over to the other side. After moving to the small Texas settlement from Georgia in the mid-1800s, the young beauty became engaged to a local man who soon went off to fight in the Civil War. More than her heart was broken when he didn't return from the war; her mind was never quite the same after that. She eventually plunged to her death in the nearby creek, but legend didn't clarify if it was by choice or by accident. Either way, caught as she was in the uncertainty of what happened to her beloved captain, the delicate apparition did little more than drift through the afterlife, searching for him.

For that reason, Hannah had never quite bonded with the elusive spirit, if such a thing were even possible. She could communicate with the ghost of Orlan Valera, to the point of holding a conversation with the spirit. Even Gouyen was capable of interacting through a series of grunts and small gifted items. Caroline, however, was a different matter. Hannah wasn't sure how to reach the sad spirit who was always searching, always mourning, her lost love.

"Caroline? I think they're serving mint juleps in the front parlor."

Hannah winced, even as the impromptu words left her lips. It had seemed like a Southern thing to say, and

Caroline was the epitome of the spoiled Southern belle from the Old South. Her golden curls were always in perfect ringlets, tied with tiny satin ribbons. Her yellow hooped skirt was so wide, it barely accommodated the walls as she floated around the inn. She spoke in soft, precise words, each charmingly slurred by a thick accent.

When the spirit didn't respond, Hannah said the only other thing that came to mind. She knew it was a low blow, but it was the one thing sure to catch Caroline's short attention span. "Caroline? I think I heard a bugle's call. There may be troops nearby. You should come see."

A wispy golden head popped through the wall of the Vaquero Room. Bare shoulders and a daring décolletage came next, followed by off-the-shoulder yellow ruffles. By the time all ten yards of her skirt were visible, Caroline's watery blue eyes were shining.

"Have you seen him? Have you seen my beloved?" Her dreamy voice was more breathless than normal. "Is it Captain Musebach's company of the Third Texas Infantry? Is he truly here?"

Without waiting for an answer, she rushed forward, straight off the landing through the gaping space beyond. Hannah knew no harm could come to the apparition—after all, she was already dead—but, nonetheless, she bit back a cry of alarm. A live person taking the same plunge would be maimed, if not killed outright.

Cradling her head with her hands, Hannah realized her headache was back in full force. She was tempted to go straight to her room and call it a night, but she still had to lock up.

A loud voice from one of the rooms drew her attention, so she stopped to listen. The voice sounded angry.

After the day's events, lingering anger and exhaustion didn't surprise her, but there was venom in this man's voice. Hannah moved closer, stopping outside the Vaquero Room.

"No! I've had it! Who does he think he is?" the voice boomed.

If she wasn't mistaken, George Hernandez and Ahman Dunkel shared the room. She wasn't certain which man was speaking, but he was clearly upset. "This isn't a game," he went on. "He's playing with people's heads and hearts, not to mention their pocketbooks."

The second man spoke in lower tones, his words too quiet to hear, but the first speaker continued adamantly, "Don't be such a sniveling coward! We have to stand up to him. We can't stand by and watch him to do it again at this tournament. It's time he was stopped."

Hannah turned away, fearing another fight among the contestants. Was it always this way? she wondered. She had always thought of fishing as a relaxing, easygoing sport, but after just one day of the tournament, she now had a different perspective.

Maybe it was the added prize money. Greed, she knew, made people do strange things. Maybe it was the lure of becoming a national spokesperson. Maybe she had brought this on herself, increasing the grand prize and turning friends against one another in the quest to win.

Why, oh why, had Sadie and Fred listened to her ideas? What did she know about holding a fishing tournament?

Hannah trudged down the stairs, belittling herself for trying to change a good thing. The current system had worked for twenty-three years, so why had she felt the need to improve it? What was that saying? If it ain't broke, don't fix it. She should keep that in mind the next time she decided to meddle with one of Wilhelmina's tried and true methods.

As she reached the bottom of the stairs, the front door opened and a woman slunk in, startling Hannah. Not only hadn't she realized Tallia Haney wasn't upstairs with her husband, but the very sight of the woman was disconcerting.

Even on her best day, Tallia Haney wasn't what most people called attractive, and this clearly wasn't a good day for her. Her long face was slightly asymmetrical, but with her frizzy mop of hair in complete disarray, her red lipstick smeared beyond the wide slash of her mouth, and with streaks of mascara making dark tracks down both her cheeks, she reminded Hannah of a Van Gogh painting. Hannah had never been a fan of Van Gogh.

Tallia dangled the ridiculous heels from a crooked finger as she crept toward the stairs. She tried flashing a toothy smile, but one side of her face appeared puffy and stiff.

"I'm looking for my husband," she said in a loud whisper. "Kent Haney?"

"Top of the stairs, first room on the right," Hannah directed.

When Tallia favored her right foot, Hannah wondered if she had encountered Leroy, the huge Great Pyrenees that came with the property. Even though the friendly white beast was harmless, his size was intimidating. More than one person had created unnecessary harm to themselves, simply trying to escape. They didn't realize the only thing dangerous about Leroy was his adoring tongue and the swish of his tail.

"Mrs. Haney?" Hannah asked in concern. "Are you all right? Can I help you in any way?"

Tears pooled in the other woman's eyes and for a moment, Hannah thought she might cry. A single tear slid down her left cheek, clearing a trail through the streaked mascara. "Honey, I think I'm beyond help."

With that cryptic statement, she limped up the stairs in her bare feet.

In her wake, Hannah caught the distinct whiff of bourbon, a man's cologne, and what smelled like dead fish. She waved the offensive scent away and moved out of its path.

At least when Caroline went looking for her man, she left behind the lingering scent of lavender.

# CHAPTER 6

The inn hosted breakfast the next morning, making it the perfect time for a briefing on contest rules and regulations. Guests were invited to join the contestants, so Hannah wasn't entirely surprised to see Tallia Haney in the dining room that morning.

It was what the woman wore that was so shocking.

Tallia had on another pair of skintight leggings, these in a leopard print. She wore a peasant-style blouse pulled low off the shoulder, revealing freckled skin and a very ample bosom. With so much cleavage showing, no one noticed the slight bruising on the right side of the face.

Even Hannah, who had made a mental note to check for signs of injury first thing this morning, forgot to immediately look. She was too distracted by the daring show of cleavage, the thinness of the white blouse, and the three-inch spike of hot-pink heels. It was all she could do not to offer the woman a jacket to cover herself properly.

Kent Haney seemed to be the only man oblivious to his wife's scandalous appearance. The moment she walked in, every male in the room was compelled to look her way. A few popped their eyes back into their sockets and looked away, either out of respect or out of guilt. Some of those stole covert glances in her direction now and then, but there were a few, a very few, who frowned at her wanton display and turned away in distaste.

Most stared with obvious appreciation, their mouths hung agape and their breath rapid. Sweat popped out on one man's brow. Another man wet his lips. At least half sucked in their guts.

Hannah was one of the very few to look into Tallia Haney's face. The redhead had tried to cover the signs with a thick layer of makeup, but even from across the room, Hannah could make out the tell-tale hint of bruising. The shape of three fingers was faint but distinct. Her cheek was slightly swollen, and her mouth sagged a bit on the side, something that may or may not have been normal. Hannah wondered if one of the reasons Tallia wore such an outfit on this day was to avert attention from her face. Even with her orange-red hair pulled into a messy bun and secured with dazzling rhinestones, with a body like hers on such wanton display, not a single man was looking at her face.

Oddly enough, Hannah noted that only one angler turned his head away from the spectacle of Tallia Haney. She happened to be watching when Rand Galloway went so far as to physically turn his chair away from the couple at the front of the room. Tallia had chosen the longest route possible through the crowd of ogling men.

"Did you see that?" she hissed to Sadie, who stood by her side.

"How could I miss it?" the older woman snorted in distaste.

"I don't mean Tallia. I mean Rand Galloway. He just got up and turned his chair around, so that he wasn't facing her. Doesn't that seem a little odd to you?"

41

"You mean, like maybe he's deliberately ignoring her?"

"Maybe. Or maybe it's the only way he can keep his eyes off her. Obviously, very few men in the room are able to do so."

"Hmm. I see what you mean. In fact, the only men not staring at her are Walker, Davy Mulligan—he's a Baptist preacher, by the way—and Kent Haney."

"And Rand Galloway."

"And Rand Galloway," Sadie agreed in a thoughtful tone.

"What do you think it means?"

"I think it means they have something going on."

"If you can manage to look past the triple D cups—"

"Oh, honey, those are at least F," Sadie insisted.

Hannah continued in a droll voice, "A mile or so north, her cheek is swollen and slightly bruised. I saw her come in very late last night, looking like something the cat dragged up. I think someone slapped her."

Sadie drew in a sharp breath. "I see what you mean."

"I also saw her in the shadows with someone at the fish fry, and it definitely wasn't Rand. Or her husband. Whoever it was, she was all over him like ivy on a pole."

"Are you sure it wasn't like a stripper on a pole?"

"That, too. But I have to say, I feel sorry for her."

Sadie jerked her attention to the woman at her side, staring at her as if she were dressed as inappropriately as Tallia. "Why on earth do you feel sorry for her? She doesn't even have enough respect for herself to dress decently, especially at eight o'clock in the morning!"

"That's just it. I don't think she has a shred of self-respect or self-dignity. She dresses like a hooker because, otherwise, men wouldn't give her a second glance. She's not exactly a beauty queen. Not that it should matter, but you know it does."

Sadie didn't look convinced, so Hannah pushed on. "And last night, when I offered to help, she said she was beyond help. You have to feel sorry for someone who has that little self-esteem."

"I suppose," Sadie admitted grudgingly. "But I still say she should put some clothes on! It's one thing to dress like that when she goes out at night, but this is breakfast, for crying out loud. I'm afraid she's going to curdle the milk."

Fred came bustling their way, her face set into a scowl.

"That woman is a disgrace!" she hissed through her teeth. "We need to take control of the situation and pull the attention away from her. Let's get the meeting started."

"But people are still eating," Hannah protested.

"It's more like they're eating their hearts out," Fred snorted. "I can't stomach so many people making a fool of themselves this early in the morning. Come on." She grabbed Hannah's hand and dragged her to the front of the room.

Hannah wasn't surprised to see the spirit of Orlan Valera sweep into the room. The ghost had a way of appearing when he was needed most. It was a good thing, too, as she still hadn't figured out how to conjure the spirits when she wanted them. It was a bit disconcerting, having spirits float in and out at their own volition, but she couldn't help but smile now. She wondered what the helpful ghost had planned as he hovered over the Haneys' table, spinning in a slow circle.

She didn't need to wonder for long. Orlan spun upward as Ahmed Dunkel passed Tallia's chair, clipping the edge of the man's elbow. Ahmed's juice glass tipped, spilling its contents over her head and sending a stream of orange down her face and neck. Tallia leapt from the table in outrage, but the edge of the tablecloth had mysteriously tangled in her bracelet. When she jerked away from the table, so did the cloth. With all its contents.

Breakfast foods went flying in all directions, splattering against Tallia's leopard leggings and her formerly pristine blouse. She sputtered in rage, her sultry, come-hither outfit now smeared with scrambled eggs, oatmeal, and a nice selection of fresh fruit.

It took a moment for her husband to stop laughing and come to her aid, but he finally sprang to action. In a clumsy and ill-fated attempt to cover her humiliation, he jerked the rest of the tablecloth free and wrapped it around her body. The act only made matters worse. Hot coffee, gravy, and pancake syrup added into the mix, creating an unsightly, sticky mess. As Kent bustled her from the room, she flung a bitter tirade of curses and insults to Ahmed, the inn, and to the very husband trying to help her.

Just before Orlan twirled his way through the shiplap wall, Hannah flashed him a look of amused gratitude. He dipped his wide-brimmed cowboy hat her way in acknowledgment, vanishing as quickly and silently as he had appeared.

With Tallia gone and the mess cleared away, Fred redirected everyone's attention to the contest at hand. She and Hannah went over the all-important rules of the tournament.

As the name suggested, there were three phases to the Hannah Trifishlon. One of the most unique aspects of this tournament was that each phase was a well-kept secret until it started. Even now, the anglers had no idea what their first challenge would be. They listened with rapt attention, hoping to detect a clue.

Before the briefing ended, Fred spoke up with a reminder.

"You have the morning and early afternoon free to do as you please. A light lunch will be served here at noon, or you may go into town. Just make certain you're on the bus by four p.m. We'll leave at promptly a quarter after and drive to our secret location, where the first phase of the contest will get underway. Guests and spectators are welcome to follow in their own vehicles, but only the finalists and contest personnel can ride the bus. Judges will also ride in their own vehicles. Any questions?"

When no one spoke up, Hannah thanked them for their attention and dismissed.

As the door to the sporting goods store opened, a bell sang out with a merry twinkle.

"I've got it," Danika volunteered, flying up from the breakroom table. She glanced at the clock. He said he would drop in around one thirty, and it was that on the dot. He was here!

Ridiculously long legs and the exuberance of youth had her at the door before the others could push away from the table. "Finish your lunch," she offered. "I'll holler if I need help."

Without waiting for a reply, she split the curtains with a graceful hand and stepped forward. The move took her from the back room into the main store, and one step closer to the man she had met a few days ago.

He was too old for her, of course. But the boys from school were just that: boys. She had a brand-new high school diploma and the world ahead of her. This man was a stranger in town, just the thing she was looking for. Distraction from the boredom.

It didn't hurt that he was nice looking, charming, and had money to spend. In just one visit, this man had already fattened her paycheck for the week. After today's visit, she knew that amount would most likely double.

She scanned the room, not seeing him. Before her stomach could sink to her toes, she heard his warm baritone.

"Well, hello." The smile was in his voice. His eyes were once again hidden behind shiny, polarized sunglasses, but she saw the way the skin wrinkled around the edges. She knew the smile reflected in his eyes, even if she couldn't see them.

"Welcome back," Danika said, trying to sound more aloof than she felt. "What can I help you with today?"

She felt his eyes travel over her, sparking flames along her skin each place they touched. He spoke not a word, but his message was clear. He was as into her as she was to him.

When he did speak, his voice was deceptively detached. "Can you tell me about these shirts?" He fingered the display in front of him.

"Certainly."

Like the first time he came in, he coaxed her away from the front counter and the security camera's all-seeing eye. Set the way it was, it caught only activity at the door and the cash register.

He stood closer than was considered polite. His sexy cologne teased her senses and whispered words of caution, but Danika tossed them away with a flick of her long hair.

"I wish I'd been able to watch that tournament you mentioned," he told her. Somehow, spoken low and close, the words sounded like a secret, shared just between the two of them. "I guess it's over by now. How did it turn out?"

"Actually, the first round starts today."

He managed to look surprised. "You don't say."

"And don't ask me for specifics. I can't give them to you," she cautioned, her eyes all but dancing.

"I wouldn't dream of it," he murmured. He crowded closer to her, a smile twitching at his lips. He gave a careless flick to the shirt on the rack. "Do the contestants wear these kinds of shirts?"

"Possibly."

"Would you say these are best suited for fishing in a lake, or a river?" he asked.

"Oh, I would definitely say a river," Danika told him. She moved to another display, to a brand that was almost twice as expensive. "But I suggest one of these. I think you'll find these offer what you're looking for."

"Really?" The creases around his eyes and mouth deepened.

"Absolutely. But I would get two, if I were you." Danika fingered the silky polyester while touting some of its best features.

His fingers brushed against hers as he inspected the garment.

"I can see the benefit of that," he said smoothly, nodding his head. "I could buy the pink one for fishing the Pedernales, or the green one for fishing the Guadalupe. Blue would be good on the Blanco River. Do you have a coral, for fishing along the Colorado?"

"I'm afraid not. I suggest sticking with the pink and the green."

He never glanced at the price tag. "I'll take them," he said.

Danika quickly plucked two shirts from the rack before retreating further into the store, pulling him toward another display. The commission on this would buy her a new outfit for Saturday night.

She gave the man a confident smile. "I'm sure you'll want one of these, as well."

# CHAPTER 7

"Blackie Cole, what are you doing here?"

The less than friendly greeting came from Fred. She charged from the office and all but plowed down the older gentleman standing on the other side of the door. What transpired was a tangle of long, flowing beard and sharp, pointed elbows. The force of Fred's body pushed against the wiry frame of his, and they both landed in a heap upon the wooden settee.

"Why, Fred," the old man squeaked, his pale cheeks coming alive with pleasure, "if I'd a knowed you was so anxious to see me, I'd've come sooner!"

The petite fireball righted herself from his lanky form, muttering something about the poke of skin and bones and how he should watch where he was going.

"I knowed where I was a'goin'," he shot back. He cupped a bony hand around his snowy white beard and smoothed downward, over and over, milking the long strands back into submission. "Twas headed into the office."

"You've got no business inside the office. It's private."

"That's why I was about to knock. Before I could get my hand in place, you bowled me over! Tweren't my fault."

"How was I supposed to know you'd show up unannounced?" Fred grumbled as she straightened her shirt and patted her coiffed hair back into place.

There was no such luck for Blackie. His thatch of snow-white hair and bushy brows were as out of control as always. When he frowned, one dipped down into the other, and resembled an avalanche of snow sliding across his forehead.

"I didn't know I had to announce my intentions of calling upon you, seeing as this is a public place of business."

Popping up from the settee, Fred countered his common-sense reply with uncommon aggravation. Blackie was a local busybody with enough time and boredom on his hands to make a nuisance of his inquisitive nature. "We don't have time for your foolishness today, Blackie Cole. But since you're here, you might as well speak up. What was so important you had to come all this way out here?"

"I thought I might throw in with the fishing tournament again this year."

Blackie and the Turner sisters shared a long history. Many years ago—Fred wasn't about to admit to the precise number—the trio had been quite the team, whiling away the hours of a restless Texas summer. Blackie was older by several years, but he allowed the sandy-haired sisters to tag along behind him. Together, they roamed the dirt roads with fishing poles in hand. More than once, they invited themselves to cross through a landowner's pasture en route to a favorite fishing hole.

Back in the day, Blackie was a formidable foe to all fish great and small. He was even a previous winner of the Trifishlon in its early days, some twenty years ago. Back in the day, Blackie had an uncanny ability to drop a line into the water and come back with a fish.

These days, his hands were too unsteady to hold a pole with any clear distinction. The wobble and dip could be from his hands, could be from a fish's nibble. Caught fishing on a windy day, his long, thin body looked frail enough to fly into the water alongside his lure.

"Throw in?" Fred repeated his words with a scoff. "How, exactly, would you throw in? The finalists have already been chosen. Not that you had a shot at making the short list, anyway, you old buzzard." There was just enough affection in the words for them to fall short of an insult.

"I may be a bit long in the tooth to compete," the old timer agreed, "but I know these rivers and creeks better than anyone. I come to volunteer my services. I could do some scoutin' or be a judge. Not for pay, mind you, but for the pure pleasure of a wet hook in the water."

In spite of herself, Fred felt her heart softening at the simple poetry in his words.

"That's mighty generous of you, Blackie. I think we've got our bases covered, but I'll mention it to the others, all the same."

"The fish have been bitin' real well 'round Trammell's Crossing. Might be a fine place to take the crew," Blackie suggested.

Fred darted her eyes about the spacious room to see if anyone was around to overhear his words. Unbeknownst to the aged angler, that was the exact location of today's competition.

"You know good and well the locations were chosen weeks ago, and are highly confidential," she said in a breezy voice. "Even if the fish are hopping straight from the water onto the stringers, we can't go off on a wild tangent and suddenly change our plans."

The old man harrumphed at her dismissal. "Trammell's Crossing should've been the plan all along," he muttered. "That, and—"

Before he could inadvertently reveal another of their chosen locations, Fred broke in. "Sadie has a fresh batch of oatmeal cookies just out of the oven. How about a few for the road?"

If he heard the subtle hint, he chose to ignore it. "I reckon I got time for a cup of coffee and a couple of cookies," he said with an agreeable smile. "Thank you for the offer."

She chose not to set him straight. Instead, she hustled him into the kitchen, where the least amount of people would overhear his musings.

She knew her old friend meant well, just as she knew to never trust him with a secret. He had generously offered his help, but if they should accept—which was doubtful—he couldn't be trusted with any confidential information. Blackie Cole was a good man, but as loose lipped as a braying camel.

"How ya do, Sadie?" he greeted the other member of the Turner family.

Sadie shot her sister a meaningful look, but she called on her good manners to greet the man with a smile. "I'm doing fine, Blackie. And you?"

"My arthritis is behavin', so I reckon I'm fine," he said, shuffling toward the table and lowering his lanky form into a chair.

The kitchen of the old inn was a study in old vs. older. There was a full-sized, cast-iron stove against one wall, the kind that burned on wood. Sadie liked to say it was more for beauty than for duty, but on cold days, or when the electrical lines went down from a storm, they sometimes cranked the old girl up and enjoyed its timeless service. A more modern-day stove sat across the room, but even it had seen better years. Hannah had tried to replace it with an energy-efficient model, but Sadie begged her not to. She had cooked too many meals and made too many memories at that stove, she claimed. She said she was too old to learn the ways of a new cooker, so unless Hannah liked her vegetables scorched and her casseroles half-cold, she should leave well enough alone. So, there it still sat, between the original farmhouse sink and the scarred old kitchen table. The only new appliance in the room was the shiny commercial freezer Hannah insisted on purchasing.

The inn's official dining area was part of the long front room running the breadth of the building. Like oldtime hotels seen in Western movies, it was an open, allpurpose space divided by ornate oak support pillars and the placement of furniture. A collection of seating options gathered around the massive limestone fireplace at the west end of the room. On the other end, past the staircase and the check-in counter with its original fretwork and vintage cubbyhole grid, were a dozen or so tables scattered about to accommodate diners.

Officially, the inn only served breakfast for its guests. It wasn't until mere days before the grand reopening that Hannah learned of the weekend brunches. Depending on the number of guests staying with them, open tables were offered to the community on a reservation-only basis. Sadie was well known for her talents in the kitchen, so there was rarely an empty seat. In fact, Blackie had been one of the first to show up when the inn re-opened, hoping for some of Sadie's delicious homestyle German dishes.

The sisters hadn't intentionally kept the brunches from the new owner. After dedicating their entire lives to the inn and their late friend Wilhelmina, they were as much a part of the institution as were the scarred wooden floorboards. They hadn't meant to act out of turn. It never occurred to either of the Turner women that they could be overstepping their bounds by assuming business would go on as usual, even with a new owner. They didn't keep details such as the weekend brunches and the annual fishing tournament and the fall hayrides from her on purpose. They simply forgot to mention something that was, to them, as much a part of doing normal business as was changing sheets and stocking fresh linens.

So while the dining room was for breakfast and brunches and the occasional hosted evening meal— although Hannah had yet to yield on that front—the kitchen was for everyday use. It was here that the women of the inn ate their meals. Here that they plotted and schemed, rejoicing when all went according to plan, and lamenting when it didn't. Here, in the heart of the inn, that Walker Jacoby often joined them for informal meetings than edged more toward personal visits. Long before Hannah arrived on the scene, the thirty-four-year-old attorney had been a staple at the kitchen table.

And it was here that friends dropped in for coffee, as Blackie did now.

"I don't care if it is a hundred degrees outside. I sure could use a cup of your fine coffee, Sadie. And a few of those warm cookies Fred mentioned would hit the spot, too, I reckon."

"I reckon they would," Sadie said with a resigned sigh. Busy or not, it went against her upbringing not to grant his request. With a single glare, she directed her sister to join them. This was Fred's doing, after all.

It wasn't that they objected to visiting with their old friend, per se. A nice little chat would be fine. The problem was that Blackie never quite knew when to say goodbye. They both had far too much to do today without entertaining a gossiping old man with time of his own to kill.

After describing his health ailments at length, Blackie turned back to the topic of fishing. He reminisced about days past and some of the good times he and the sisters shared in their youth. Without encouragement, he then offered his opinion on the best bait to use at all his current favorite fishing holes. Hannah came into the room as he extolled the virtues of crank bait on an open-face reel.

"Hello, Mr. Cole," she greeted.

Taking full advantage of the interruption, Fred flew to her feet. "Oh, my word! Look at the time! You don't have to say another word. I know I'm late. I'll be right there." She managed to look appalled at her alleged tardiness.

Hannah caught the pointed look in her eyes. After the slightest hesitation, she thought to nod and play along. "I, uh, wondered what the holdup was."

"T'were me, I'm afraid," Blackie said, taking full responsibility for the blunder. He pushed slowly to his feet, his actions accompanied by the pop and sigh of aging limbs. "I was jawin' and lost all track of time. Me an' the girls were moonin' over some of our favorite fishing holes back in the day."

"I believe you mentioned a few of those the last time you dropped by." Hannah graciously left out 'and the time before that, and the time before that, as well.' She hid the silent thought behind a tolerant smile.

"I was tellin' the girls," he went on, completely blind to the fact that neither woman had been considered a girl in over fifty-odd years, "the fish are hoppin' around Trammell's Crossing. A'course, in the middle of the day the water's so warm they come out half-cooked, but the evenin' is a fine time to wet a hook."

Hannah made a strangled sound of surprise, but Blackie never noticed. He clicked his tongue, shaking his white head with regret. "The honey holes have done gone sour on Lake Buchanan and parts of the Llano. The ghosts are all riled up again, so they've been scarin' the fish away, right and left."

Hannah's head jerked up in surprise, then pivoted from Blackie to Sadie, and then to Fred. "Th—The ghosts?"

"Not all ghosts are as sweet and pretty as yours is," the older man all but scolded. "Some are downright ornery, peeved to have their souls left behind when their bodies have done turned to dust. And some still have vengeance in their heart."

Hannah shook her head, starting out with a denial. "I only know about our—" She caught herself before she said something she would regret.

She knew it was foolish on their part, but none of them would openly confirm Blackie's claims of seeing ghosts on the property. They ignored any reference he made to the apparitions, neither denying nor affirming his statements. To some measure, it was their own warped version of 'don't ask, don't tell.'

"I... don't know what you're talking about," she amended.

"That pretty little gal who floats around here in the yellow dress. Most of the ghosts 'round the lake were farmers and dressed in work clothes. Haven't seen a single one of them in a yellow dress."

Eager to change the subject, Hannah glanced down at her watch. "I hate to cut this short, Mr. Cole, but we have an important staff meeting starting in less than five minutes. With so much to do with the tournament, I'm sure you understand."

"I sure do, young lady. Don't pay me no never mind." He waved a shaky hand in the air. "I'll finish up my cup of coffee and be on my way."

"Absolutely. Have a nice day."

"We'll be right there, Hannah," Sadie assured her. She pulled the plate of cookies away, but not before their guest snagged two more.

"And don't forget," Blackie added. "If you need another hand, I'm your man."

Hannah knew it wouldn't be necessary, but she smiled and thanked him, all the same.

# CHAPTER 8

By four o'clock, Hannah was seated on the bus with eleven of the twelve finalists, plus the official alternate. For this first contest only, should one of the finalists be disqualified for any reason, the alternate could step in and participate.

Sydney Branch still hadn't arrived. Missing the bus was definitely reason for disqualification.

With two minutes to spare, Sydney raced from the inn and jumped aboard the bus. Hannah didn't think his feet even hit the first step as he leapt inside.

"Did I make it?" he panted, breathing heavily.

Fred consulted her watch. "Just barely. You had exactly one minute and forty-three seconds before the ax fell."

Relief flooded into his flushed face. "But I made it," he said with reverence.

Fred nodded her gray curls. "You made it."

He sauntered down the aisle, his attitude losing its humbled spirit. He beat his chest and released an exuberant battle cry. Most of his colleagues shared his enthusiasm, but a few looked disappointed.

"Did you see that?" Hannah whispered, leaning in toward Fred.

"See what?"

"His shirt was all rumpled, his hair messed up, and I could swear that's a smear of lipstick across his upper lip."

"Stripper pink?" Fred guessed. It was an apt description of the color Tallia wore this morning, before wearing her breakfast.

"Exactly."

Fred pursed her lips in thought. "Sydney is a worthy opponent for any man here. I wonder if Tallia was a deliberate distraction."

"You think she was deliberately trying to make him late?" The very thought startled her.

"It was a common enough thing in the rodeo. Buckle bunnies would distract other riders, hoping to throw them off their game to give their man a better shot at winning."

"That's unscrupulous, on so many levels."

Fred shrugged her slender shoulders. "I'm just saying I've seen it happen."

Hannah studied the faces of the men on the bus. "Kent Haney doesn't look too happy," she noted. "It could be because he, too, suspects Sydney was with his wife."

"Maybe. But most of his death glares seem to be directed at Rand."

Hannah scanned more faces. "Melvin Maddox doesn't look too happy, but then again, I doubt there's much that does please that man. Gil Mendoza definitely isn't happy, because this is his only shot at making the tournament. The only other people not passing out high fives are Sly—"

"Jealous, perhaps?" Fred suggested.

"You think?" Hannah asked in surprise.

"It's always possible."

"I suppose. And Rand. He doesn't look too happy, either."

"We had this discussion earlier. Like Kent, he may suspect Tallia was with Sydney," Fred pointed out.

As the bus rumbled to life, and the driver pulled away from the inn, Melvin Maddox was the first to ask, "Now can you tell us where we're going?"

Seeing no reason to keep it secret any longer, Hannah stood at the front of the moving bus and spoke, "And we're off! The first phase of this year's Hannah Trifishlon is officially underway. First stop, Pedernales River to do a little fly fishing!"

An excited murmur moved through the bus. Hannah gave them a moment to express their approval before she continued, "Naturally, Luckenbach Poles will supply all your fishing tackle for the day. Everyone will fish with the exact same rig, exact same bait. It will be your individual style, knowledge, and natural talent that will set you apart from the crowd.

"Normally when people think of fly fishing, they think of trout. But this evening, we'll be fishing for largemouth bass. There is a five-bag limit. You are not allowed to catch and release. You catch it, you weigh it. We'll be fishing again tomorrow morning at a different location. Same rules will apply. The eight fishermen with the heaviest bags will go on to the second round, meaning that four of you will be out after tomorrow morning."

Hannah motioned to her friend with a smile. "I'll now turn the questions and concerns portion of this over to my esteemed colleague, Miss Fredrika Tanner."

Again, Melvin was the first to speak up. "Why did we wait so late in the day to get started?"

"As you know, Melvin, the best times to fish in this heat are during the cooler portions of the day. In Texas in July, those are few and far between, but early morning and late evening are the best bets. So no sleeping-in tomorrow morning. Next question?"

"We can't use our own flies?"

"Not unless you want to be disqualified, George. Next?"

"What if we don't want to keep one of the fish we catch?"

"You heard what Hannah said, Peanut. You catch it, you weigh it. Anyone caught releasing a fish will be disqualified."

"Can we find our own spot along the river, or are they pre-determined?"

"Good question, Sly. As long as you stay within eyeball distance of a spotter, you are free to find a favorite spot along the river. First seed has first pick."

"Who are the spotters?" Rand wanted to know.

"Anyone wearing one of these bright green Team Hannah t-shirts," Fred replied, indicating the shirts she and Hannah wore. "Believe me, these shirts are so bright, even the fish will be able to see us."

"That's what I'm worried about," Melvin groused. "You'll mess up our fishing."

"That sour attitude of yours will mess up your fishing, Melvin. It may just turn the water."

"That's another thing," Sydney called out. "We don't have waders."

"Thanks to Johnson City Outfitters, that's not a problem. Tell us your size, and we can get you fitted right now. We have the gear with us."

The hour drive passed quickly as they passed out boots, exchanged one size in favor of another, and listened to the excited chatter of the fishermen around them. Soon they were pulling into the Pedernales Falls State

Park. A string of vehicles pulled in behind them, carrying spectators, spotters, and judges. Tallia Haney was conspicuously absent.

As everyone gathered alongside the bus and awaited their equipment, Judge McNutt went over the rules again. He spoke loudly enough that everyone, including the spectators, could hear. There were specific rules for onlookers, including distances they were required to keep and invisible lines they couldn't cross.

Davy Mulligan was asked to say a prayer for their safety and sportsmanlike conduct, and with that, the contest began.

By special arrangement, the area of the park where they fished was closed to the public. That allowed only the contestants and their fans to make the three-quarter-mile trek to the river, where they could have an almost two-mile stretch of the river to themselves.

The park itself was over five thousand, two hundred acres of pure, natural beauty. Named for the Spanish word meaning flint, it was an apt description for a river carved into layers of flint and stone. The formation of the river and its natural boundaries were a geologist's dream. The formations were millions of years in the making: 115-million-year-old Cow Creek limestone to form the sharp and fissured bluffs; Cretaceous layers to form the flats; the Marble Falls cherty limestone of the Pennsylvanian age, some 320 million years old, to create the main cascades. The dark gray Marble Falls limestone was finely grained but embedded with resistant chert, or silica. With its partial reinforcements and crinoid fossils, the limestone had eroded into beautiful and interesting forms. Through the centuries, the constant onslaught of rushing water had carved the stones with distinctive pits, fissures, and potholes. Most potholes—formed when eddies swirled into the rock and ate away at the stone in a circular pattern—were horizontal, but the park was known for one particular large, horizontal pothole on a boulder wall.

Trammell's Crossing was a low-water crossing that allowed easy access into and across the swiftly moving ankle-deep waters. From there, the fishermen could easily wade into the stony riverbed of the Pedernales. If they preferred fishing from the banks, either side of the river had ample sandy, flinty, and often rocky shores on which to stand.

Hannah observed from the banks, delighted with the raw beauty surrounding her. The water was clear and tinted green, colored by the reflection of leaves and lush foliage. Even in many of the deeper spots, she could see straight to the bottom, including the fish that swam there. Huge cypress trees, towering ash, and buttonbush edged the water, in some places thick enough to obscure a clear view of nearby anglers. The official spotters adjusted accordingly, keeping tabs on their assigned fishermen.

It was more than just the beauty of the area. Hannah was equally enthralled with the beauty of the sport. She understood now that fly-fishing was an art, just as Wilhelmina and the sisters claimed. There was pure grace in the way the anglers cast their lines, in the way the nylon zipped through the air and landed upon the water. Hannah reminded herself she was there to spot errors and questionable practices, not to ask questions or get lost in the beauty of a cast. She bit back squeals of excitement when the anglers pulled a wiggling, dancing fish from the waters.

As a city girl, she was still adjusting to the idea of touching the fish, but she decided if she could milk a cow and gather eggs, she could unhook a fish from a line.

However, she underestimated how much the fish would fight when she unhooked her first one and almost lost it. She grabbed its slippery scales with both hands and hauled it against her unceremoniously, much to the amusement of Sydney Branch. As long as she didn't lose his catch and got it to the scales, he didn't mind her bumbling efforts. In fact, he told her she was kind of cute with her flushed cheeks and her unveiled enthusiasm.

Suspecting he had cavorted with Tallia Haney mere hours before, Hannah was unimpressed with his efforts to flirt with her. She gladly drifted on down the banks of the river, where she kept a loose eye on Sly Patterson and George Hernandez.

"Enjoying yourself, Miss Duncan?" George called.

"Yes, I am!" she answered with a genuine smile.

Sly stood closest to her. With a nod in Sydney's direction, the female angler offered a quiet piece of advice. "Watch out for that one."

Hannah's dark hair whipped in the wind as she jerked around to study the man she had just helped. "You think he's cheating?" she asked in surprise.

"Not in the contest," was Sly's cryptic reply.

As dusk crowded in, the judges called the fishermen in for the day. A few had reached their limit and watched from the rocky banks, but some were still in the water, trying to get that last bite.

"We'll post Day One weights when we get back to the inn," Hannah told the group as they boarded the bus. "Good job, everyone! I hope you enjoyed it as much as I did."

Everyone seemed to be in good spirits as the bus lumbered back to the inn.

"That was fun," Hannah told Fred as they settled in for the ride. "I stink to high heaven and have fin cuts and possibly fish guts all over my hands, but I had a great time!"

"It was a nice day, wasn't it?" Fred smiled.

"Best of all, everyone seems to have mellowed. Even Bart Hinkle acted decent today."

"He's not really so bad, just a hothead. And like everyone else, he has it in for Rand. Poor Rand, being first seed, he always has a target on his back."

"He seems to take it all in stride, though. Even though everybody seems to be angry with him, I seldom see him lash back."

"Why should he? He's riding high in the rankings. Not just here in our little tournament, but nationally."

"He seems like a nice enough man."

"He is. Like most of them, he's trying to get to the top in a sport he loves."

"Hey, I did pick up on one thing today." She leaned in closer to confide, "I think you were right about Sly. I think she's involved with Sydney, or at least she wants to be."

"I agree, but what made you decide that?"

"He tried flirting with me, and she made some cryptic statement about him being a cheater, but not in the contest. I had the distinct feeling she meant he was cheating on her."

"Worth keeping an eye on."

Hannah up straighter. "Why? You think there's trouble ahead?"

Fred patted her arm with an indulgent smile. "Sweetie, Sadie and I have been doing these tournaments long enough to know there's always trouble ahead."

# CHAPTER 9

Sadie led a string of smiling children away from the barn, listening to their happy chatter.

"Wait till I tell Dylan Dewberry what I just did!" one boy boasted, a proud grin stretched across his freckled face. "He won't believe I milked a cow, all by myself!"

Sadie could dispute the last part of his assertion, but she chose to remain silent.

"That was awesome," a little girl at her side beamed.

"I thought milk came from the grocery store," another girl confessed. "I never knew it came from cows."

"Just wait until you taste it," Sadie told them with a smile. "I'll have it chilled and ready for you in the morning. It goes perfectly with the eggs we gathered."

Leroy danced in and out among the group as they talked excitedly about today's adventures.

"I thought for sure Henny Penny would peck my hand, but she was really gentle," a second boy said.

While the fishermen and their groupies had their

excursion at the river, Sadie led a different sort of excursion for the children staying with them. Sadie's *Farm Day Adventures* was all about life in the country. With the aid of her helpers, she shared the joys of living among nature with the children.

For the summer, Hannah had hired several local teenagers to fill the gaps within her staff. Dawson Gaines and Brianna Kohl were two of the best, and both had volunteered to assist with Sadie's day camps.

Brianna signed up because she loved animals. This fall, she would attend Texas A&M University and study veterinary medicine, bringing her one step closer to her dream of becoming a vet. She enjoyed being around children and got a kick out of the way the little girls already idolized her, imagining themselves in her shoes one day. For her, this was the perfect summer job, and the last one she would hold before going off to college.

Dawson signed up because he loved Brianna. He had never been courageous enough to ask her out in high school, but he realized their days together were numbered. In just a few short weeks, she would be in College Station, and he would be in Abilene. If spending more time with her meant putting up with a dozen whiny kids and their relentless questions, so be it.

He had finally gotten up the nerve to ask her out, too, but that was before that fishing guy had shown up. Now she was all doe-eyed over the dude, and all but ignored Dawson. Three days ago, she had laughed at his jokes and suggested they hang out after work; now she was always on edge, waiting for a glimpse of *him*.

Barely even two days, and the man already had her wrapped around his finger! It was enough to make a guy sick.

Dawson knew better than to let his annoyance with the fisherman show. The boss women had already given the staff instructions. Anything the semi-pros wanted or needed, they had to provide. This week was all about them. In essence, the staff had to all but wipe the anglers' butts for them. That was his interpretation of the orders, anyway.

But it was a job, and his dad was always on his case, saying he needed to make his own money. He said baseball was a fickle sport, that a bruised shoulder or an inflamed wrist could be the difference in winning and losing, of going pro and going home. Having a job wasn't about the pay; Dawson's dad was a bank president, and his mom was from 'old money,' whatever that meant. Dawson didn't need a job to have spending money; he needed one to prove he knew the value of hard work and dedication. Even a dead-end job like this one made his parents happy, and it gave him something to do until he was off to college for fall practice.

Plus, it gave him time to win over Brianna. Dawson wasn't particularly crazy over all the kids, but they seemed to like him, and he knew it made a good impression on her, whether she admitted it or not. Electronic devices were strictly prohibited during Sadie's Farm Adventures, so they filled the hours with low-key, organic fun. And Dawson was nothing if not a fun guy.

While the sun was high in the sky, they stayed indoors as much as they could. Dawson had a good singing voice and knew a few simple strands on the guitar, so he entertained the group with sing-a-longs and silly lyrics. What Brianna lacked in talent, she made up for with enthusiasm. Miss Sadie had cratefuls of arts and crafts projects, so Dawson pretended not to mind the sticky fingers and the streaks of paint and the silly paper hats, because the hokier the craft, the more Brianna laughed. She wore every macaroni necklace and every pirate hat the kids gave her, and she made Dawson wear them, too. If it meant she stepped close enough to wrap her arms around his neck and tickle his nose with the essence of her strawberry shampoo, he had no complaints. He wore them all with a goofy smile, because it was something the two of them shared.

Most of all, they shared their love of the outdoors. And everyone agreed that the best part of the adventures was the time spent outside in the fresh air and sunshine.

The children especially enjoyed interacting with the animals. Not only did they learn how to feed the chickens and gather eggs, the youngsters were also able to pet and feed the goats. Under close supervision, they learned to saddle and brush down the horses. Dawson and Brianna helped them into the saddles and led their mounts around the corral by the reins, giving them a taste of how it felt to ride a horse. And now, with the day drawing to an end, they learned how to milk a cow.

Some of the children were from the city and had never seen or been around a farm animal before. They delighted in the velvety feel of a horse's nose, giggled at the wiry hair twirling around the goat's horns, and squealed beneath the rough scrape of a calf's tongue. For Sadie and her helpers, this was what the day was all about. Seeing their enthusiasm for nature always lightened Sadie's heart and put an extra spring in her step.

The animal's unique names always made the children laugh. The chickens were named after a nursery rhyme, the horses after country music singers, and the cows after ice cream flavors. The goats sported names like Mary Poppins, Captain Hook, Ariel, and Steve Urkel, borrowed from favorite literary and media characters.

"I love Buttercrunch!" the first little girl said, her dark eyes dreamy. "Her hair was so soft. Just like Leroy's." She ran her hand through the white shag of the dog's fur, comparing it in her mind to the cow.

"But her nose was wet!" another child giggled, touching his own in comparison.

"I wish we lived here. Then we could visit the animals every day."

"It is pretty cool," Brianna told them with a smile.

"Living on a farm is hard work," Sadie told them. "What you see and did here today is on a very, very small scale. Imagine if we had dozens of chickens, or hundreds of goats. Some farms have pigs. And many farmers raise gardens and crops, meaning there is much more work to be done. Can anyone tell me some of the crops farmers raise?"

Some of the guesses were wild. One boy thought they raised wool, straight from the ground. The first little girl guessed flour. Sadie took time to explain how each answer could be considered correct, in a roundabout way.

While she explained how another guess, corn-bread, was a by-product of farm crops, Dawson found his way to Brianna's side.

"Hey," he said, trying to sound causal, "I was thinking about going to *Ringo's* when I get off tonight and grabbing a burger and float. Wanna come?"

The hum of a motor drew their attention. Brianna's eyes lit up as the rented shuttle bus lumbered its way up the gravel road, stirring up a plume of dust in its wake.

"I, uh, I'm not sure," she hedged, her eyes darting from the bus to the boy, and back again. "I may have other plans."

Dawson's eyes narrowed. He would bet those plans revolved around the fisherman, and whether he had time to encourage the teenage girl. Brianna was way too young for the jerk. And why was he interested in her in the first place? He obviously had something going with the long-legged woman. That lady was homely enough to scare children, but Dawson had to admit, she had the body of a goddess.

In his eyes, Brianna was the goddess. She was smart, beautiful, and way too young and innocent for a

69

guy like the fisherman. The old guy had to be at least in his thirties. Flirting with the eighteen-year-old might be legal—*barely*—but it was still disgusting.

He thought about saying something to Miss Hannah about it, but he didn't want to get Brianna in trouble. What if the boss blamed her, thinking she had encouraged the old guy? She might fire Brianna, and then he'd lose his chance to be with her.

This was probably something he should handle himself. He was busy trying to decide just how he would handle it—go to the guy directly, go to the woman in the skimpy outfits, or do something less direct, but just as effective—when he realized Brianna was looking at him, waiting for his reply.

"Whatever," he said, shrugging as if it made no difference to him. "I may ask some of the others if they wanna go."

"Cool," Brianna said, but her eyes had drifted back to the shuttle.

Disgusted, Dawson made his way to Sadie's side. She, at least, appreciated him and whatever help he offered.

"Let me take that for you, Miss Sadie," he said, reaching for the small container she carried. He and Brianna always carried the larger containers of fresh milk. Normally, he offered to carry Brianna's load, but he wasn't feeling so generous this evening.

"Why, thank you, Dawson," Sadie said, relinquishing her hold on the milk. "How kind of you."

As they walked from the barnyard toward the inn, Sadie had a limited view of the RV pads and the five rigs parked within them. Three of the RVs were large and showy; the other two were smaller, lower-end versions of semi-luxury travel. All were decorated with stickers, decals, and insignias identifying their rank and association with the fishing industry.

However, it wasn't the RVs or their stickers that caught Sadie's attention. Instead, it was the two women slipping through the shadows surrounding the parked vehicles.

One woman wore skimpy clothing and three-inch heels. The other wore a flowing yellow hoop skirt. Not only were the images complete opposites, but neither should have been at the RV site.

She made a mental note to mention the incident to Hannah.

They had little say over where Caroline wandered, but Tallia Haney was another matter.

# CHAPTER 10

By the moon's mellow glow, Caroline slipped between the trees. After noticing the strange train cars earlier in the day, she was drawn to the massive iron contraptions. How did they travel without a steam engine? Where was the caboose? Unlike the black iron bodies she was accustomed to, these were shiny and bright, in a rainbow of colors. She couldn't resist coming back for a closer look.

In all the time he had been gone from her, she had received but a single letter from her betrothed. She had misplaced the yellowed pages long ago, but even before that, the letter bore a permanent crease from constant folding and unfolding. With or without the physical pages, Caroline could recite each line by heart. The four-page correspondence was the one thing that tied her to her precious Ezekiel, and the closest thing she had to holding a conversation with him.

Within those pages, Ezekiel described traveling by train to meet up with other Confederate troops. Could *this* be his train? Could Ezekiel be aboard one of these odd-looking cars? Had he returned to her, at long last?

Instead of being strung together as a whole, they were lined up side-by-side. She tried to make sense of their idle positions. She peered around, over, and under them all, noting how their normally spiked and sparse wheels were bloated and full. Was the light colored one on the end the caboose? The placement was right, but she didn't see the familiar smokestack.

After a long inner debate, Caroline drummed up the courage to look *inside* the cars. Manners dictated that she knock, even though no one answered. They never did.

As a last resort, she finally decided to slip inside. It was the only way she would know for certain if Ezekiel were there.

In the first car, the small light-colored one, Caroline saw two men, but neither was her betrothed. One man lounged across a lower bunk, lazily thumbing through a magazine with fish on its cover. The other sat at a small table, stringing a fishing pole with line while sipping from a shiny silver can. Both were too old, too heavy, and frankly too lazy to be her dear soldier. Her Ezekiel was tall and lean, with a head full of dark wavy hair and a lively, energetic approach to life.

The second car was close to the same size, with a single man inside. Caroline didn't linger long. She could see his bald head above the covers as he snored in his bed.

The middle train car looked more like the sleeper cars she was accustomed to. It had two sets of bunks and a wide, fluffy bed with its own private quarters. But a family resided within the confines, including four boisterous children.

Naturally, she and Ezekiel had talked of the family they would one day have together, but there hadn't even been a wedding yet. Nor a wedding night.

Moving along, Caroline pushed her head through the shiny chrome of the next-to-last car. This looked more like the dining car, with its elaborate kitchen. It had a large table with a cushioned bench curled around it. There was a fluffy divan and a proper door into a separate compartment where—

*Land sakes alive!* Caroline pulled back, aghast at the improper display of naked flesh and skimpy clothing. She didn't want to see anything more. *That* man, the one with the hungry leer upon his face as he cavorted with the scantily dressed woman, was definitely not her captain!

Discouraged, Caroline moved to the final car. If she didn't find her beloved here, she would have to start over again.

The interior of the last car was dim. She suspected the occupants might be asleep, but she heard a voice. It slurred softly with a Southern accent, but the tone wasn't as deep as Ezekiel's. Still, it was worth a listen. Caroline pushed further inside.

"I don't care what we have to do. We have to stop him."

Could this man be referring to a Northern general? Sherman, perhaps? The despised leader scorched his way across the South, burning everything in his wake. Did the man inside this car intend to stop the vicious plundering of homes and towns? Folks said that, before he threw his devastating torch, Sherman took anything of value. Caroline had heard the whispers, the horrid accusations that the plundering often included women and children.

The man spoke into a thin, rectangular box that he held to his ear. The strange device was similar to the ones she saw most people with these days. The little boxes held their attention for hours upon end and rarely strayed from their sight. Whatever the thing was, it was highly valued in today's society.

"But you have the advantage of home field," the man said into the box. "We can't let him win."

*He was!* Her heart sang out. *This man was plotting*

*his strategy against Sherman!* Somehow, the little rectangular box helped him develop a plan of action against Northern troops. Caroline wondered if Ezekiel had a similar tool, and if he used it now, to find his way back home to her.

Her mind refused to acknowledge what some had so cruelly whispered behind her back. There were those who claimed Ezekiel would never come home. That he was buried in a foreign field, lost to her forever. She knew it wasn't so. He had *promised.* He promised he would come back to her, and that they would marry and have a life together. Captain Ezekiel Musebach was as honest and good a man as ever lived. He never lied, and certainly not to her.

So, if this man in the strange-looking train fought on the same side as her dear soldier, and if he plotted to win the war against Northern aggression, she would listen, and she would help; not because she supported slavery, but because she supported Ezekiel. She didn't believe in the right to own slaves any more than he did. In fact, most everyone in and around the German settlement opposed slavery. While many of their neighbors refused to take up arms, Ezekiel fought because he felt it was the patriotic thing to do, despite her objections. He said it was a matter of principle, a matter of the North dictating to the South. But in her humble opinion, it was no different than the slave owners dictating to their slaves.

Not that anyone had ever asked her thoughts. She knew women weren't supposed to have an opinion in political matters. They were told what to think by first their fathers, and then their husbands. Women, like children and pretty baubles, were best appreciated when seen and not heard.

However, they were in the midst of a war, and special times called for special measures. All efforts were appreciated now, even those by women.

While Caroline was woolgathering, the man continued speaking into the box. She missed most of what he said.

"I'm depending on you."

She caught that much, at least. And what other field could this man be speaking of, if not the battlefield?

While Caroline pondered the question, the man dropped the box from his ear. It went dark, no longer shining with its colorful inner lights. Then the man shivered slightly and reached for the bed covers, muttering something about a chill in the air.

When he rolled over and lay his head upon his pillow, Caroline knew there was nothing else to hear.

She slipped out of the odd sleeping car and made her way through the trees, careful to stay away from the creek that ran nearby. She didn't remember the exact details, but something horrible had happened at that creek. Just going near the creek filled her with an immense sense of grief and despair.

The memory was vague, but she recalled venturing near the dark, rushing waters on a dark and moonless night. There had been days of hard, non-stop rain, until the rivers and creeks were swollen with dark and swirling waters. On that night, she felt compelled to visit, drawn there by some unknown urgency. She remembered crying. She remembered clutching something in her hand, a letter bearing the insignia of the Confederate States of America. She couldn't remember what was in the letter—didn't *want* to remember the terrible lies it told—but she remembered thinking if she could just make it to the creek, her troubles would be eased.

South Grape Creek was their place. She and Ezekiel would meet there, beneath the sheltering arms of the live oaks and the ash trees. It was there that he stole his first kiss. There that he first asked her to marry him. There that he broke her heart by announcing he had joined the fight against Northern aggression. And it was there he had kissed her that final time and promised—sworn, even—that he would return to her. Caroline didn't remember *why* she felt the desperate need to go there that particular night, but she knew it pulled her there with a force greater than herself. Whatever happened there left her feeling cold and empty.

For that reason, she avoided the creek now. It was no longer *their place.*

Taking the high road away from the creek, Caroline ignored the gaggle of young men gathered around their rides. She remembered carriages looking different from these shiny adaptations. She wasn't sure when, but over time, the shapes and sizes of wagons and carriages had shifted, morphing into these strange, unrecognizable vessels.

While Caroline was lost in her broken heart and troubled mind, so many of the things she recognized had changed, if not disappeared altogether. Quite without her knowing it, the world had turned into a different place. Homes looked different now. People dressed differently and spoke differently. They definitely acted differently!

These young men were a perfect example. Once upon a time, boys were taught to be gentlemen. She remembered a time when simply the presence of a lady would be enough to have these young men standing at attention, minding their tongues and their manners. At least one, if not all three, would have rushed to her side, offering his arm as she crossed the uneven lawn. Good manners wouldn't allow them to ignore her and her treacherous plight through the darkened path. Yet, there they stood, still laughing and talking about a plan to get even. Plotting some nefarious deed to put another someone 'in his place.'

Caroline passed within three feet of the boys, and not a one of them acknowledged her.

Fanning her flushed face with her exquisite ivory and lace fan, Caroline mourned the days of her youth, when gentlemen knew the proper way to treat a lady.

# CHAPTER 11

He had learned long ago that fishing was a ritual-istic sport.

It wasn't just about talent, as some would say.

It wasn't just about method.

It wasn't just about rigging.

It was as much about ritual and tradition as it was anything.

To that end, he wore his same lucky shirt, no matter how many new ones he bought.

He wore the same pair of socks throughout a single tournament, no matter how horribly they smelled.

He insisted upon the same battered, sweat-stained, misshapen hat.

Pretty or not, once he started a tournament, he didn't shave for the duration.

He methodically went through each step now, making certain he adhered to the time-honored traditions. He couldn't afford the smallest of oversights. Not with so much on the line.

He was *this* close to having it all!

The cash prize was nice, but the spokesman gig was a game changer. Tallia craved fame and attention above all else. If he couldn't give her the world, he could at least give her fame.

Tallia deserved it. She had had a rough life, but she was the kind of woman who never gave up. She made lemonade from life's lemons. Found silver in every dark cloud. She might take a tumble, but she always came out on top. Like him, she was a fighter. And a winner.

They deserved to win. His life hadn't been the proverbial bowl of cherries, either. It had been more like the bowl of pits, but that was all about to change. This one tournament could make the difference and put him over the top, once and for all.

Most of all, he would be top in Tallia's eyes. It was the ultimate prize.

He pulled on his favorite fishing shirt and settled the battered hat atop his head. Scratched his stubbly chin and sniffed his socks, determining they hadn't quite ripened yet. Pulled them on slowly, one smelly, prickly inch at a time.

Superstition, some called it.

He called it taking no chances.

# CHAPTER 12

The sky was still dark when the bus pulled away from the tiny hamlet of Hannah. Sadie, along for today's excursion, handed out breakfast burritos and fresh fruit as the fishermen came aboard. Fred doled out cups of hot coffee, and Hannah offered bottle water.

"Today," Hannah told them as they settled in for the ride, "we are fishing for rainbow trout in the Guadalupe River."

An excited murmur moved through the bus.

Despite the Texas Parks and Wildlife Department's aggressive stocking program for rainbow trout, the scorching summers were too brutal for any measure of large-scale success. Some of the released fingerlings migrated to other rivers and creeks, but for the most part, the waters were too warm for their liking. The exceptions were in select pockets of the Guadalupe, where the waters were cool enough to support the species year-round. The river was the only one known for its wild-born rainbows and brown trout.

By the time the bus reached its destination, the

first rays of the sun streaked across the sky, painting it in soft pastels.

The river welcomed them with the thick, moss-draped arms of bald cypress trees. Giant specimens of the stately old trees hugged the banks, some of them tall and straight, others bent and stretched out across the water. At random intervals, impressive limestone bluffs edged the winding waterway. The river swirled and eddied around big rocks and tiny falls, rushing to sweep the rocky bottom of the river with a current that was lively and quick.

The morning sun skipped across the water and danced amid the currents, making Hannah feel alive and invigorated. At most, the water reached only as high as the fishermen's waists; it struck them mostly at mid-thigh or lower. Random rocks and boulders created a natural obstacle course in many places, and more than once, Hannah used the jutted stones to walk out across the river.

Perhaps it was because today was a new day.

Perhaps it was because the magic of surprise had worn off.

Perhaps it was because the fighting spirit of the trout stirred a similar spirit within the anglers.

Or, perhaps, it was because today marked the end for four of the contestants.

Whatever the reason, the camaraderie of the previous day had disappeared. Despite the beauty of early day and the pleasant morning temperature, attitudes were sharper today. Fuses were shorter, allowing tempers to flare more easily.

Peanut Ayers insisted he saw Rand flick a small trout back into the waters.

As Jimbo Thompson moved downstream, Butch Tanger staggered into the waters, claiming Jumbo pushed him.

According to George Hernandez, Billy Joe Claus intentionally snagged his line with his, scaring off a large brown.

Melvin Maddox kept a close eye on Melinda Benswanger, maintaining the sexist judge favored the lone female contestant.

From behind the invisible barrier, Bart Hinkle was once again his normal self, finding exception in everything the anglers did, particularly Rand Galloway.

In accordance with state law, all rivers in Texas were accessible and open to the public. When entered at a public access point, once in the river, a person could theoretically navigate the waterway for its duration. Getting *out* of a public thoroughfare river was the tricky part; if the land surrounding it was private, trespassing laws applied and were vigorously enforced. Without express permission from the landowner, a person would be forced to stay in the river until the next public access point, which in many cases was miles and miles away.

For purposes of the tournament, Walker had contracted with the necessary landowners along the Guadalupe to grant access in and out of the river. With only a specific area of the river available to the anglers, access for their audience was limited even more. Not all spots along the banks were user friendly.

Tallia had graced them with her presence and was dressed even more inappropriately today, as if to erase the memory of yesterday's fiasco. She appeared in short, white shorts and a blue polka-dotted bikini top, barely covered by a flimsy blue cover-up. She paraded back and forth along the banks, clearly distracting the fishermen. Despite the judges' calls for absolute quiet, she kept ooing and ahhing with every cast and every catch.

Hannah had finally had enough. She pulled Sadie and Fred aside and fumed about the needless distraction. "This is ridiculous! Has anything like this ever happened before? Is there any way we can ban spectators?"

"We *could*," Fred said with clear reluctance, "but

it would definitely be as a last resort. This is what the community, both local and within the fishing circuit, likes best about the tournament. It makes them feel a part of it, and—"

"—creates excitement and interest in next year's event," her sister finished for her. "It would be difficult to call a halt to it in the middle of the day."

"But she's distracting the men!"

"Just a minute. I may have an idea," Sadie said. She pulled away and picked her way toward Tallia, who stood in a provocative pose just beyond the invisible line of separation. She stood behind her husband, but her eyes were on every move that Sydney Branch made. Some of her facial expressions as she watched him were better suited for an X-rated movie, a fact not lost on Sydney or Sly, who fished just upstream.

Sadie spoke with Tallia for a moment, gesturing to the grass between them and the riverbanks, and once, toward Hannah and Fred. They had no idea what Sadie told her, but they watched as the scantily dressed woman recoiled in horror and jumped several feet backwards. She then retreated even further, taking high, widely spaced steps with her four-inch heels and long, spiky legs. She didn't stop until she reached a picnic table set some thirty feet off the riverbank. She crawled atop the table and sat with her long legs folded beneath her, well beyond the fishermen's view.

When Sadie returned, they asked what she had said to produce such impressive results.

"Oh, I just mentioned that you two had seen several snakes among the grasses, but you lost sight of them just before they reached where Tallia stood. It didn't take her long to decide she would watch from a distance for the rest of the morning."

Hannah laughed in delight. "Perfect! Now if it would just work on Bart Hinkle!"

"If I remember correctly…"

"It's spiders he's afraid of, more than snakes!" Fred recalled.

"Sister, I think it's time you did spider surveillance. Pretend you're following a big, hairy tarantula and lose sight of it when you reach ol' Bart. That should get rid of him, at least for a while."

"Speaking of surveillance, I guess we should return to our posts," Hannah told her friends. "Fred, find a spider on your way back. Be sure and squeal when you spot him."

"Even if I don't," the gray-haired spitfire predicted with a wink, "I'm sure Bart will."

C

With Bart Hinkle and Tallia Haney effectively silenced and well behind the invisible barrier, the rest of the morning looked promising. Hannah was lured into a false sense of security until a half hour before their scheduled departure.

The anglers were strung up and down the river within the specified range. Rand, Jimbo, and Ahmed had wandered to the far northern end of the spectrum, with Walker volunteering to keep pace. Without disturbing the water, he scrambled around huge cypress trees and their long, gnarled roots, worked his way over rocks and sand, and, from the banks, trekked parallel with the fishermen as they waded the shallow riverbed.

Walker knew there were those who claimed that fly fishing was part witchcraft, part art form. As he stood watching Rand Galloway effortlessly cast his fly, he had to agree with the old adage.

Like any expert fly fisherman, Rand observed his surroundings and imitated them to the best of his ability. As bugs rose and lit on the water surrounding him, he flicked his line just so, matching the direction of the wind, and the length of his line with the depth of the water. Ever so precisely, with the quick, silent weightlessness of a dragonfly, he laid his bait upon the riffles. The whispered landing didn't produce as much as a splash.

It happened all at once.

The smooth surface of the water broke.

The fly disappeared.

The line jerked.

Downriver, a strangled cry penetrated the stillness of the morning.

Walker ran toward the sound of distress, skimming tall grasses, twisted roots, and the unexpected jut of cypress knees. He raced around a slight bend in the river, trying to make sense of the scene before him. A pair of feet dangled several feet above the water, twisting and turning in a vain attempt to touch bottom. Jimbo Thompson appeared to suspend in midair, just beneath a cypress limb stretched low across the river's edge. The man clawed at his throat, trying to convey his frantic message in a voice hoarse and breathless. As he spun once again, sunlight glinted off the razor-thin filament string wound snugly around his neck.

Walker grabbed his two-way radio, barking out instructions for an ambulance and immediate help. Without slowing as he ran, he scanned the area, looking for options on how to get the man down. All the while, he wondered how a cast had gone so terribly wrong. Surely, an experienced fisherman like Jimbo Thompson knew not to throw without overhead clearance. How had his line managed to tangle and pull him along with it?

Reaching Jimbo at last, Walker tugged on his legs, but a croaked cry told him the movement only made matters worse. He would have to find another way.

The trees along the riverbanks were old and giant. With trunks forty inches in diameter and their lowest limbs eight feet or more off the ground, climbing the cypress wasn't an option. The nearby tree, however, grew at an odd angle, its massive arms leaning over the river.

Without missing a beat, Walker scrambled up the trunk, until he was within jumping distance of the tree where Jimbo dangled.

Urging the other man to hold on—begging him not to give up hope just yet—Walker hurled himself into the air and crashed into the heavy arms of the cypress. He missed the first limbs he grabbed for. Scraped against prickly branches and spiky needles. Knew the sickening sensation of a free fall. Found a handhold, just as he re-signed himself to a sudden and hard fall.

Walker worked his way through the tree, swinging and climbing amid the tangle, when he heard another hor-rific cry. It came from ten or so feet downriver, as Ahmed Dunkel crashed through the water, coming to the aid of his fellow angler.

Peering through the foliage, Walker saw Ahmed flailing about in the river. This scene made no more sense to him than when he first saw Jimbo. Instead of wires in the tree, Ahmed appeared caught in wires in the water.

But no. Those were too thick for wires. Too dark. Those were...

Snakes! Ahmed had stepped into a nest of water moccasins in the water!

From where he was in the tree, there was nothing Walker could do for the second man. But he could still help the first man, whose whimpers grew fainter and hoarser. Wincing with empathy for Ahmed and yelling out for more help, Walker frantically pushed his way to Jimbo. He still dangled from the limb by a fishing line.

Even now, Walker couldn't make sense of how such a scenario could take place.

Rand raced past them to help Ahmed. George Hernandez rushed in from the other side. Together, the two men found a sturdy fallen limb to extend into the water toward the terrified man.

Walker didn't have time to watch the scene un-
fold. He had his own emergency to deal with.

Jimbo had worked his fingers between the fishing
line and his neck, but the thin line sliced into his skin, doing untold damage to the digits. Blood ran down his hands
and onto his arms. Walker reached into his pocket, but as
he pulled out his knife to cut the line, he heard the first
crack.

Another crack, and the limb broke free. It all came
crashing down: the limb, the tangled man, and the rescuer.
The trio splashed into the water before either man had
time to react. Relishing the temporary reprieve, Jimbo
sputtered and gasped, thankful to hit the rocky riverbed.
He struggled into a sitting position, his head sticking
above the shallow water as he greedily gulped in air, but
the rushing current wanted to take the limb with it. Each
tug tightened the line still wrapped around his neck.

Walker was keenly aware of his own tenuous position. A seven-foot limb pushed against his chest, trying to
fight its way down river. The man tied to it by his neck
was little deterrent for the force of nature. Mere feet behind them, the water was alive with a dozen angry snakes,
striking out at anything that dared intrude upon their nest.

Timing was of an essence. He heard the others
shouting. Some were on the banks behind him, trying to
save Ahmed. Others ran their way, eager to assist him
with Jimbo. But there was no time to waste. Walker had
to move quickly if he were to save himself or the fisherman.

With a sure hand, he sliced through the line with
his pocketknife, setting Jimbo free. The man's fingers
were badly damaged, and he had trouble pulling air
through his windpipes, but he was free.

"One of you get Jimbo, one of you help me with
this limb!" Walker called to the rescuers splashing nearby

into the water.

Behind him, Ahmed had managed to drape himself across the proffered limb. Several men tried pulling it to shore, none of them quite heroic enough to step into the waters and risk snake bites of their own. Walker knew that releasing this first limb wasn't an option, no matter how difficult it was to hold steady in the swift current. If he lost his hold, the broken limb would carry downstream, knocking Ahmed back into the snake-infested waters. He couldn't possibly survive such an outcome.

By the time Peanut and Sydney waded in to help wrestle the limb and Jimbo to the bank, the other crew had pulled Ahmed to the shore. Snake bites pocked his face and arms, and he was a ghastly shade of white.

Hannah burst onto the scene, several of the spectators and spotters not far behind. She spotted Walker splashing from the river, dangerously close to where a few snakes still angrily struck at the water. Their eyes met, and she would have raced to him, but he waved her off with a cautioning hand. He staggered from the water, physically drained despite being soaked through and through. His shirt was ripped and plastered against his chest, but Hannah was too frightened to appreciate the way it molded around his muscles. Amid multiple scrapes and scratches, a thin streak of blood working its path down one cheek, and great, heaving breaths, he was nonetheless on his feet and doing far better than either of the fishermen.

"These men need immediate care," he called, stopping her in her tracks. His blue eyes conveyed a silent message. *I'm okay. They're not.*

She wanted to touch him and reassure herself he was safe, but she knew he was right. Her first responsibility was to the fishermen, particularly in the condition each was in.

"EMS is on its way," she assured them. "We have

two ambulances coming. Do we need a third?" This question was directed to Walker.

"I'm good," he insisted. He fell onto the bank beside Jimbo, where he went to work trying to comfort the writhing man.

After the ambulances came and carted the men away, and after Hannah and her team rounded up the emotional contestants and bystanders and herded them all away from the river, Walker stayed behind.

First, he pulled out his phone and took pictures of everything he saw. Next, he called the sheriff's office. He knew they had been alerted to the accident, but he wasn't sure that was the best way to describe today's events.

Neither incident felt like an accident to him.

They felt more like attempted murder.

# CHAPTER 13

Team Hannah did their best to keep spirits up and confidence high as the bus shuttled the solemn group back to the inn. Competition or not, it was an emotional time for the other finalists.

For the most part, the fishing circuit was a small community, and the members were friendly, if not true friends. In the space of a single afternoon, two of their own might never return. Ahmed clung to life, while Jimbo faced possible permanent damage to his hands. Their comrades were left walking the fine line between sorrow and relief; they felt terrible for their friend's fate, but they knew it could easily have been them in those ambulances. Survivor guilt rode alongside them on the bus.

Lunch was a solemn affair. Cold subs and sandwiches fed appetites less than hearty. Soon after eating, everyone scattered to their own corners.

Hannah spent much of the afternoon on the phone, getting updates on both men's statuses. It came as no surprise that Ahmed was listed in grave condition. Flown to Houston for specialized treatment, it was still too early to predict whether he would survive. Jimbo was transferred to a San Antonio hospital and underwent emergency surgery. Although the extent of his injuries was still unknown, he was expected to recover.

After some debate, they decided to go forward with plans for their evening meal. Originally planned as a celebration for the eight fishermen headed to Round Two, Hannah and her team used the opportunity to bolster spirits and to announce a change of plans. Bag weights were announced and ranked, but, due to the day's tragic turn of events, the judges voted against eliminating anyone. All ten contestants would compete in tomorrow's contest.

Compliments of tournament sponsor *Matousek's Market,* the fishermen and their families enjoyed a huge spread of German meats, sides, breads, and beers. It helped boost morale and put a positive twist on a day gone horribly wrong.

Hannah was still smiling when Walker pulled her aside, saying they needed to talk. Detecting the solemn note in his voice, she felt some of her optimism slide.

"I'll slip out and wait for you in the church courtyard. Join me when you can," he said without explanation.

The quaint, white clapboard church was at the far end of what Hannah jokingly referred to as the 'town green.' The lone road in the tiny town forked around a large grassy patch where a trio of massive old live oaks stood. The shaded area added distinction and charm to the dusty little town, hence its nickname.

The church stood in the distance, apart from the weathered buildings edging either fork of the road. Behind the church was a small courtyard and beyond that, the trail to the Turner cabin.

Walker waited for her on a small stone bench tucked beneath an arbor of wild roses. The faithful Leroy curled by his side. Both stood when she arrived. The old-fashioned gesture brought a smile to her face, reminding her of the sad lack of manners in today's world.

"Have a seat." Walker motioned to the bench behind him.

It was a beautiful evening, studded with stars and a light breeze. It was easy to imagine he asked her here with romance on his mind, but one look into his solemn blue eyes dispelled that notion.

Her smile drooped. "What's wrong?"

Leroy dropped down to lounge upon her feet. Walker took his place beside her before answering. "We need to talk about this morning."

She looked at him sharply. "Have you heard something more? Has Ahmed gotten worse?"

"Not that I'm aware of. But there's something you need to know."

When he didn't immediately elaborate, Hannah prodded him with, "Which is?" When he scrubbed the back of his neck, Hannah recognized it as his signature stalling technique. "What is it, Walker? Just tell me," she ground out.

"There's no easy way to say this, but... I think today's accidents weren't accidents, at all."

Her voice rose in confusion. "What are you talking about?"

He pulled out his cell phone, opened the photo app, and presented it to her. "I've looked at this from every angle. Considered just about every possibility. And there's just no way Jimbo could have tangled his line badly enough to hoist himself up there."

Hannah looked at a dozen or so photos, including two sent to him by someone else. These showed Jimbo still strung from the limb, with Walker precariously poised above him. One caught the exact moment the limb broke, and the startled look on Walker's face.

"What am I looking at?" she asked, unable to

93

make sense of the photos.

"See how this limb is slightly bent? It turns upward here at the end. I think there's a fishing line there, we just can't see it. I think it was booby trapped to pull someone—Jimbo, as it turned out to be—up and into that tree."

"But…why?" she asked in utter bewilderment.

"To eliminate someone—anyone, perhaps—from the tournament."

"But that's… that's… that's horrible!"

His dark head bobbed in agreement. "I think the limb was initially sweeping the ground, anchored in a way that, when a certain trigger was released, a noose fell down from the tree, and this limb swept upward, carrying Jimbo with it." Walker pointed to the photo with his finger, tracing the chain of events as he believed they happened. "I can't believe this is his own fishing line around his neck, although I have no proof. His pole was swept downriver and could be halfway to the Gulf by now."

A look of disbelief struck Hannah's face. "You're saying someone sabotaged the tournament?"

"It looks that way." His own face was grim. "Jimbo is too good a fisherman to make that sort of mistake. He would know not to throw an overhead cast beneath a low-lying limb. He might cast sideways, but never high overhead. He wouldn't get tangled up like that."

Hannah gave a small shake of her head, still not convinced.

Walker pressed on. "Think about it, Hannah. How could his own line whip around the limb, wrap around his neck a couple of times, and jerk him up ten feet in the air? It's just not possible. There had to have been a booby trap."

"Did you find it? Did you call the sheriff?"

"A deputy and I spent an hour or more looking for

evidence. Unfortunately, it all washed downstream when the limb broke. We managed to keep the limb from interfering with efforts to rescue Ahmed, but once he was free, we let go. Most of it slipped back into the river and floated away." He paused, trying to recall if he had seen anyone help it along its way. At the time, he hadn't realized it held vital evidence.

"So, you don't know this for certain?"

"No," he admitted. "But I'm confident I could build a solid case on probable cause, alone."

"You're pressing charges?" she gasped.

He was quick to set her straight. "I'm not pressing charges. I'm just pointing out that the law of nature proves my theory is correct."

"But who would do this?"

"I don't know. But I think they're responsible for the snake nest, too."

Hearing his latest accusation, Hannah shook her head vehemently. "No! That can't be! How and why would someone do that?"

"Why? For the same reason they booby trapped the tree. To eliminate another fisherman, and to increase their own odds of winning."

"And how? How would they manage to get that many snakes in the river? To make them stay in one spot, the exact spot that Ahmed just happened to step in?" Her eyes snapped with indignation; not at Walker, but at the very idea he presented. She couldn't believe someone could be so vile.

"I don't know the particulars," he admitted. "I imagine they used some sort of live trap with a delayed release mechanism. The snake nest wasn't more than fifteen or twenty feet from the tree. Either one could have triggered the other. All I know is that yesterday morning, and last week, and the week before that, when I scouted the river and used sticks along the banks to see if any snakes stirred, I only rustled up one single snake. Except for a hole here and there, the river is clear. Clear enough to see to the bottom. I never saw a thing. I find it hard to believe that a nest of fully grown water moccasins set up housekeeping overnight, in almost the same spot as that booby-trapped tree." The adamant tone of his voice matched the hard set of his mouth. There was no doubt of his assuredness.

Hannah sat in stunned silence, nibbling at her lip. She had difficulty wrapping her head around his assertion, yet a part of her knew it was so.

"I did this," she whispered at last.

"What?" He whipped his gaze around to her and saw the guilt that flooded her face. She looked completely stricken. Understanding what she meant, he wrapped his arm around her waist and spoke to her in a soft but firm voice.

"No, Hannah. You didn't do this. You are not in any way responsible for the reprehensible actions of others."

She pulled away from his comforting touch. "I did! I did do this!" she cried insistently. "I increased the jackpot and finagled *Luckenbach Poles* into offering the spokesman gig to the winner. I encouraged greed and competition, and now two men are hurt! Ahmed is fighting for his life. If he dies, his blood is on my hands!"

"Hannah, honey, that just isn't so." Walker grabbed her hands and held them within his. He leaned in closer, forcing her to acknowledge him. "Look at me. Look into my eyes and listen to me, Hannah." His voice was gentle but insistent. "You didn't do this. You are not to blame."

"I am!" she wailed. Tears dripped over her lashes to spill across her cheeks.

"No. This is the work of someone who is greedy and malicious and cruel. You are none of those things.

96

You could never deliberately hurt someone."

"I didn't do it deliberately," she agreed, sniffing back more tears. "But I caused them to be hurt."

"Then I'm just as guilty. I'm the one who suggested you contact *Luckenbach Poles* about their fishing poles. Are you saying you blame me for this?"

"Of course not!"

"Then it's Sadie and Fred's fault, huh? They liked your idea of upping the prize and went out and found several new sponsors. So *they* did this."

"Now you're being ridiculous!" Hannah snapped. "Of course it's not their fault."

Walker's eyes glowed in the semi-darkness. "That's my point," he agreed gently. "It's not their fault. Just like it's not your fault."

Unwilling to concede the point, Hannah simply changed the subject. "Who did those things, Walker? Who could want to win so badly that he would stoop to such means?"

"I don't know. But whomever he—or she—is, we're going to stop them."

She eyed him skeptically. "You think Sly is behind this?"

"At this point, I don't know what to think," Walker confessed. Now that she had calmed a bit, he took another chance at putting his arm around her. This time, she leaned into his warmth, and they settled more comfortably upon the bench. "We can't afford to rule out anyone," he said.

"If this had happened yesterday, Gil Mendoza would be the top suspect. He was still in the running then, but I think we can mark him off the list now."

"Not necessarily," Walker contradicted. "If I'm right about the booby traps, it means someone knew our location before we announced it. I don't know how they discovered it, but what if someone—Gil, even—thought we would visit the Guadalupe first? What if this was supposed to have happened yesterday?"

"Then, Gil could still be a suspect," she agreed. "But how would someone know our locations? We keep those top secret until the very last minute."

"It could have been a chance encounter. Somehow, someone overheard something they shouldn't have, and word got back to the wrong person. I'd like to think it was an innocent leak."

"And if it weren't?"

"Then one of the judges or someone affiliated with the contest leaked confidential information." Simply saying the distasteful words left a sour taste in his mouth and curled the edges of his mouth downward.

"I don't like that possibility."

"Nor do I. We can circle back around to that problem later, but for now, what do you know about the rest of the contestants? Gil isn't the only one with a motive. Potentially, every single one of them has motive."

"Maybe not Jimbo and Ahmed," she murmured. "If so, their plan backfired terribly. As for the others… yes, I'd say they all have motive. Rand, I suppose, is the least likely to sabotage the contest, given that he's firmly in the lead."

"It's possible the attack could have been intended for him, I suppose." Walker considered the possibility aloud. "As first seed, he had choice of location. It makes sense that he would go as far upstream as possible, closest to the hole."

"Again, who would do this? Even though Bart Hinkle and Melvin Maddox both love to complain and could easily fit the profile of a sore loser, I have trouble imagining either one of them as a potential killer."

"Long ago, I learned that you can't judge a person's guilt or innocence by looking at them. Often, even the people closest to them don't recognize the danger signs."

A shiver walked down her spine. "Are we putting the rest of them in danger? Should we cancel the tournament?"

Walker again rubbed the back of his neck. Even without the visual signal, the worry was evident in his voice. "I've been asking myself that very question. The deputy didn't seem overly worried. Unless we find a trap, there's no way to prove or disprove my suspicions about the snakes. Even the booby-trapped limb could, theoretically, have been a terrible accident. I still think it required more than Jimbo's cast, but there could have been old lines dangling from the tree... a snapped limb... Stranger things have happened, all perfectly innocent but deadly, just the same. Without clear intent, it's one thing to *suspect* foul play. It's another to prove it. By canceling the tournament without valid cause, we would open ourselves up to a potential lawsuit."

"But we can't risk any more lives! What if this was deliberate, and the guilty party strikes again?" Hannah nibbled on her lip for a moment before asking, "Is it too late to change our location for tomorrow?"

"Probably."

"If someone *did* leak information about our secret locations and intended methods, changing them up at the last minute would surely foil their plans."

"While I agree, I don't think it's possible at this late date. We have multiple locations tomorrow, accessed in most part by private land. I've already secured all the necessary paperwork to waive issues of trespassing, legal responsibilities, insurance claims, and such. To round up new permissions before tomorrow would be almost impossible. Not to mention that our sponsors have gone to the effort and expense to provide the necessary equipment and riggings for phase two. We can't just change horses in the middle of the stream." With a slight frown, he added, "No pun intended."

"But what if something else happens?"

"I shared that concern with law enforcement," he assured her. "Their advice was to remain extra vigilant tomorrow and stay alert to the first signs of danger. At this point, there's no proof that today was anything more than a terrible and unforeseen accident."

Hannah's reply was a pronounced frown.

Walker took her hand in his and squeezed, his other arm still around her back. "Given that we have a contractual agreement with the sponsors and the contestants, and we have no evidence to back up my suspicions, I agree that our best course of action is to stay alert, stay vigilant, and to report *any*thing questionable."

Hannah lay her head against the comfort of his shoulder. "I suppose it's a good thing we aren't allowing spectators during this next phase of the contest. That should be of some comfort."

"Agreed. The fewer people around, the better. Not only for their own safety, but it helps with means and opportunity."

"And today?" she wondered. "Who had the means and opportunity?"

"I think the bigger question is, who had the knowledge and foresight to do such a thing? It would be someone who knew where the contest was taking place. There weren't many people privy to that information."

"The four of us," Hannah agreed, referencing herself, Walker, Sadie and Fred. "Sadie and Fred were in charge of coordinating with the sponsors to supply the needed equipment for each phase of the tournament. If they discussed location, I know they used discretion and urged the vendors to do the same. They've been doing this long enough to know the ropes."

"That leaves the shuttle service and the landowners. There's no way of knowing if any one of them could have mentioned their involvement, but it's unlikely they had contact with the contestants."

"Are any of the contestants local?"

"A few are from the general area. Billy Joe Claus is from Horseshoe Bay and Davy Mulligan from the Bulverde area. Sydney Branch is originally from Llano, but he moved to Lake Sam Rayburn when his fishing career kicked off."

"You forget. I'm from Houston and don't know the area. Are those places near here?" Hannah asked.

"All are within an hour or an hour and a half of here. Except for Lake Sam Rayburn," he added. "That's over in East Texas, about four hundred miles from here."

"So, even though Sydney lives there now, he has ties to the area. Feasibly, any of those men could have connections to our sponsors and our locations."

"And to the staffs of such, including yours," Walker pointed out.

"You know I have a *very* small staff. Sadie and Fred, one part-time employee, seven teenagers for the summer, and I use contracted cleaning services. There's the off chance that any one of them could have overheard us mention the location, but it's doubtful. If anyone knew the location before this morning, it could have been some of the teens working the kitchen, helping Sadie prep for breakfast. But," she added, "I rather doubt any of them would have much interaction with the fishermen."

"That still leaves the staff of our associated partners."

"So our pool of suspects—for lack of a better word—is growing, not shrinking," Hannah moaned.

"Don't get discouraged. We'll figure this out." He squeezed her hand for reassurance.

"Thank you, Walker."

He gazed down at her with a bemused expression. "For what?"

"For all you're doing. You've always been involved in the inn, but you've gone above and beyond for the Trifishlon. Not only are you a judge, but you've been a scout, a coordinator, a fundraiser, and now, you're even an investigator." She lifted her face and smiled at him. "I couldn't do all this without you, and I want you to know how much I appreciate it."

"You know I'm fully vested in the inn," he assured her, but there was a warmth in his voice, and in his eyes. "I'm not just the executor of Miss Wilhelmina's will and overseer of the trust she left behind. I was a close friend to her, and I'd like to believe I'm a close friend of the current owner, as well." His eyes warmed even more as they dropped to her mouth. He brushed his fingers along her cheeks. "You know I gave up that silly pretense of ours being strictly a professional relationship, weeks ago." He gave a slight shake of his head, as if marveling at his own inadequacies. "Despite my best intentions, I can't seem to keep my distance."

Hannah all but snorted. "Really? Because you seemed to have done a good job of it this summer. I've hardly seen you." Her words ended with a slight whine.

Walker's fingers slipped into the dark tresses of her hair. "Hannah?" he murmured.

She swallowed, realizing how close he was. Close enough that she could feel the warmth of his breath feathering across her skin. A husky note replaced the whine. "Yes?"

"I'm here now. The moon and the stars are out. And we're all alone, for the first time in weeks." He slid his arm further along her waist, tugging her closer. "I finally have a chance to kiss you. Do you really want to spend these few stolen moments talking?"

# CHAPTER 14

The next morning, there was good news coming from the hospitals. Jimbo came through surgery with less damage than originally feared. Ahmed made it through the night, and, although he was in a medically induced coma, he showed minor improvement.

After a good night's sleep and upon hearing the positive report, the mood at breakfast was optimistic, if not quietly upbeat.

Even Tallia had toned down her wardrobe for the day. Generous glimpses of skin still showed, but she wore a denim cover-up over her short shorts and low-cut blouse. If not for the bright lipstick, high heels, and her slow, sultry strut to the front of the room, she might have slipped in without a commotion.

Just in case, the wispy spirit of Orlan Valera stayed close. More than once, Hannah saw Tallia shiver and pull her cover-up closer about her to ward off the un-explained chill at her table. Little did she know that a ghost sat alongside her in the chair, making certain she felt his presence.

Hannah and Fred addressed the anglers and their guests, waiting until everyone had gone through the buffet line before speaking. Fred went first.

"Good morning, contestants! I know we're all relieved to hear promising news on Jimbo and Ahmed's conditions. After a good night's sleep and a hearty breakfast, I hope you're all ready to do a little fishing; the second round of the Hannah Trifishlon takes place today! Unfortunately, because of the location and for the safety of all concerned, spectators will not be allowed to join us today."

A rumbled of protest moved through the room, but Hannah ignored it and spoke above the grumbling.

"Today, we will be fishing for the official state fish of Texas, the Guadalupe bass. They may be small, but I understand these fish put up quite the fight! This is catch and release only, so our judges will accompany you to weigh and record only the Guadalupe bass that you catch. By the end of the day, we'll be down to our final four contestants. Those four will go on to compete in Round Three and will be eligible for the championship."

"We don't need to remind you," Fred told the group, even though she proceeded to do so, "that the Championship Grand Prize is the coveted position of becoming the official spokesperson for *Luckenbach Poles,* one of the hottest up-and-coming poles on the market today, as well as *ten* thousand dollars!"

Hands shot up, and a few called out questions, but Fred waved them off. "That's all the information we're sharing for now. Once we're on the road, we'll give you final instructions for the day. For now, enjoy your breakfast and get ready to catch some Guadalupe bass!"

They left the dining room amid murmurs of surprise and speculation. After yesterday's events, the staff took every precaution to keep today's location and method under wraps until the last moment. They couldn't allow anyone to sabotage another stage of the contest, if that was indeed what had happened.

The *how* and the *who* still haunted Hannah. *How* had they managed it? *Who* had leaked the information? Was there a particular target in mind? Most of all, *who* had done such an awful thing?

She hadn't slept well for worrying about the situation. Was there a would-be killer among them? Would he—or she—strike again? Hannah vowed to do everything in her power to keep her guests and staff safe, but it was easier said than done, especially when she fought an unknown enemy.

Hannah wandered into her office, where she plopped into her chair with a heavy sigh. They were one-third of the way into the tournament. Part of her was tempted to call the whole thing off, but Walker had a point. They had an obligation, both legally and honorably, to the sponsors who had spent their time and money to make this event happen. It would be far easier to refund the contestants' entry fees than it would be to repay the sponsors for all they had done. Their time, effort, energy, and enthusiasm couldn't be recouped.

The one thing she could do, Hannah determined, was to figure out who the guilty party was and stop them before they acted again.

But what, really, did she know about any of them?

Hannah pulled out a notepad and jotted down the names of all twelve finalists, adding Gil Mendoza and Bart Hinkle for good measure.

Sydney Branch was young and good looking. There was no doubt he was a flirt, openly flirting with Hannah and with contest judge Melinda Benswanger, not to mention both Sly and Tallia. He seemed to have something going with both, which in itself was questionable. Plus, he had ties to the area. Had he somehow used his charm to give himself an advantage in the competition?

There was something about the man…a bit too much confidence, she thought. A touch of arrogance. Maybe he thought he was above suspicion. Maybe he didn't trust his own natural talent. With a twist of contemplation upon her lips, she placed three question marks beside his name.

Rand Galloway was a bit of a flirt, as well. Perhaps it was because of his age—she judged him in his early to mid-forties—but Hannah didn't think his flattery was sexual in nature. It felt like a natural extension of his charismatic personality. Besides, why would he sabotage a tournament where he was heavily favored to win? This felt more like an act of desperation. He earned only one question mark.

She didn't know much about Sly, other than she had worked her way up the ranks in what was traditionally considered a man's sport. Such a feat took dedication, determination, and detail, not to mention a good dose of raw talent. In her desperation to succeed, would the lone female go to extraordinary measures to win? After a moment of hesitation, Hannah awarded her two marks.

Melvin Maddox claimed Sly used that status to her advantage, influencing the female judge. According to Walker, Melinda was fair and unbiased, so she didn't see Sly having much luck there. Melvin was a hothead and a grump, but he struck Hannah as being too lazy to do much more than complain about his competition. Booby trapping the massive tree at the river would have required hard work and a level of precision. Simply not fitting the mold, he only earned one question mark.

Their other hothead, Bart Hinkle, didn't fit the mold, either. Most of his ire was directed toward the lone female contestant. Angry or not about being disqualified, this sort of vindictiveness was over the top for anyone but a psychopath. Just one mark for him.

Billy Joe Claus lived within an easy drive of the area and could, conceivably, have friends, relatives, or contacts nearby. Those contacts could be involved in the contest in some capacity and have intimate knowledge of the contest locations. That, surely, was enough for one question mark. The older gentleman hardly seemed a cold-blooded killer, but she supposed he might need an edge against the younger contestants. With reluctance, Hannah added a second mark beside his name.

There had been a tense moment at the river yesterday when Butch Tanger claimed Jimbo pushed him into the water, but did that make him a suspect? Unless there was already a feud brewing between the two men, a flare of temper didn't indicate guilt. And there hadn't been time, nor opportunity, between the alleged shove and the accidents to suggest Butch's involvement. Still, the confrontation earned him two question marks.

Davy Mulligan was a preacher. Hannah knew that didn't eliminate him, but it *should*. Idealistically, no man of the cloth would ever consider such a despicable act. Considering that he had his wife and four children along with him, she temporarily dismissed him as a suspect, giving him only one mark.

Would the same mentality apply to Peanut Ayers, she wondered. The seasoned fisherman seemed to be affable enough. In her estimation, he earned only one mark, and a weak one, at that. Plus, the older gentleman had his wife along with him.

As did Kent Haney, but Hannah wasn't as quick to discount his innocence. She was ashamed of herself, questioning why she didn't allow him the benefit of the doubt. Just because his wife was… loose… didn't mean he was capable of committing such a horrific deed. He might be guilty of nothing more than loving his wife, fidelity or not. He seemed to be a quiet, low-key sort of guy and the opposite of his flamboyant wife. Knowing very little else about the man, she awarded him only one question mark.

Hannah didn't know which man she overhead

within the Vaquero Suite, but either George Hernandez or Ahmed Dunkel had expressed definite anger with someone. If Ahmed had acted on his anger, he had been a victim of his own malice. And if it had been George? Hadn't he been angry with one of the other fishermen over some alleged transgression? Again, the time and opportunity to carry out a plan of revenge didn't match up, but she was running out of likely suspects. If for no other reason than that, Hannah gave him two marks.

That left Jimbo and the first alternate, Gil Mendoza. She put an X beside Jimbo's name, just as she had beside Ahmed's. And Gil? She gave him one mark for the obvious reason that he would benefit most from the removal of another contestant. Perhaps he didn't know the rules of the contest: a substitute was allowed prior to the end of the first fishing day only. Had the accidents taken place on the first day, he would have made the cut.

Thinking of her conversation with Walker, Hannah agreed it was possible that Gil got his days and locations mixed up. Perhaps he thought they would fish the Guadalupe the first day. If that were the case, he earned another question mark.

The more Hannah thought about it, the more she suspected Gil could have been one of the men in the shadows after the fish fry. She thought it was his voice she heard accusing Rand of playing dirty. With a nod of confidence, she added the third question mark beside his name.

She looked back over the list, circling the names with two and three marks. These were the people she needed to pay close attention to. Gil and Sydney were the most suspicious of the group, followed by Sly, Billy Joe, Butch, and George.

*Good grief!* She fretted. That was six of the thirteen. With Jimbo and Ahmed out of the pool, it was six of eleven. *Half!* Half of the finalists were viable suspects in the unconscionable acts against their peers.

The knowledge made Hannah's heart heavy as she stuffed her notepad into her desk and prepared for phase two of the contest.

# CHAPTER 15

Once on the bus, they revealed the day's itinerary.

"Today's destination? The Llano River!" Fred announced from the front of the shuttle. "Best way to do it? In a kayak!" She threw her arms up in a gesture of excitement.

The feeling caught and traveled around the bus, creating an energetic buzz. It was a far cry from last night's bus ride home.

"These are the rules, so listen closely," Fred called, quietening the murmurs. "All fish must be caught while inside the kayak."

"There is a five fish limit," Hannah continued. "However, they must be the Guad only. No other fish counts. When you land a fish, alert the judge so he can officially weigh it, record it, and release it."

It was Fred's turn in their tag-team presentation. "There will be a three-hour time limit. We are fishing within marked boundaries. Anyone straying beyond the boundaries will be immediately disqualified."

"Also," Hannah cautioned, "if you leave your boat for *any* reason, other than in spots too shallow to navigate or at your official rest stop, you will be disqualified."

"Those are the official rules."

In tandem, the two women added, "No exceptions."

Never one to miss a chance to criticize, Melvin Maddox cranked up a complaint. "It's July. The river's bound to be down. I don't relish the thought of draggin' a kayak over the low spots in this heat."

"And for that reason," Hannah assured him with a tempered smile, "we'll have staff on hand for portage."

Having foreseen this as a potential problem, Walker suggested they have some of the summer help from the inn wait at the low stages of the river, ready to assist if need be. The teenagers followed behind in the second shuttle, riding with the judges.

Blackie Cole was also on that shuttle.

Allowing all ten finalists to compete in the second challenge had presented a new problem. Originally, they planned for two groups of four to kayak the river, each accompanied by a judge. Walker and Alonzo vanCleef agreed to do the honors.

Putting five kayaks in the river was bundlesome enough. The judges would have to navigate among and between the contestants; six kayaks at a time would never do. The two additional contestants meant they needed a third group and a third judge.

Hannah was reluctant to recruit the older gentleman, but Sadie and Fred had spoken up in his defense. If there was anyone who knew the river and the nuances of kayak fishing for the Guad, it was Blackie Cole. He might be full of hot air and gossip, but when it came to fish, the man knew his topic. Plus, he was available at the last minute. With her friends touting his virtues, Hannah agreed to invite him into their fold. She only hoped he would keep quiet with his ghost stories and unsolicited fishing advice.

111

The day began smoothly enough. After getting the anglers outfitted and deposited in three locations along the river, Hannah and Fred assigned the teens to their appropriate stations and helped set up the areas.

It was a good day for fishing. The fish were biting, so the fishermen could be selective in which ones they chose to weigh.

Walker had his hands full with four anglers in his charge. He paddled steadily from one boat to another, weighing and recording the fish before releasing them back into the water. The other two judges each had three contestants in their groups. By luck of the draw—Fred divided the groups by order in which they descended the bus—Alonzo had an easygoing group, Blackie had the troublemakers, and Walker had the rest.

In contrast to the rivers of the last two days, the Llano was more challenging. The terrain felt wilder here, and less serene. At this section of the river, the banks were low and less defined, melting away into the flat, rocky terrain of adjacent ranchlands. Even with a recent rain, in many places, the water fought for the right to cut along the fluted limestone bottom, littered as it was with boulders and sandy silt buildups.

As Melvin predicted, some of their time was spent in portage. Concrete low-water crossings accounted for some interruptions traversing the river; shallow water and low flow accounted for others. In such places, energetic helpers from the inn were there to do the tugging and pulling, portaging the kayaks from one water hole to the next.

Dawson was one of the summer crew members who had signed up to help. He and his buddy Ryan thought it would be a fun, easy way to earn their paycheck for the day. Except when helping the pampered finalists move their kayaks, they could spend most of the time wading into the clear, swallow waters of the Llano, sitting

112

beneath the prickly shade of cedar and mesquite, and sunning atop a flat, sun-bleached rock.

Best of all, the day offered a chance to get even with *him*, the angler who had caught Brianna's attention. Dawson had seen them just last night, lingering in the darkened shadows behind the old dance hall. Brianna had twirled her hair and giggled, acting like some silly girl in junior high, not the eighteen-year-old woman that she was. And the old man—at least *twice* her age, Dawson was certain—had grinned and looked at her like she was the coolest thing since the electric fan.

It was enough to make a guy puke. But that was okay, because today, he had a chance to get even. As luck would have it, Dawson was porter for the segment of river *he* was fishing. And while the boss ladies may have instructed them to handle the anglers with extra care, they hadn't said a thing about how to handle the kayaks. If, say, a certain kayak took an extra hard bump in portage… and if a drain plug somehow was loosened… it wouldn't be directly disobeying orders. These sorts of things just happened at the river.

As the anglers drifted toward the official rest stop they manned, Dawson and Ryan pushed to their feet and greeted the group with affable smiles. They waved and called out all the right greetings. *How's the fishing been? Caught any good ones?* Indigenous to Texas, the state record Guadalupe bass was only 3.71 pounds. *Break any records out there, fellas?* they asked.

Walker's red kayak was the first to reach the concrete barrier of the low water crossing. As he unfolded himself from the craft, he smiled and nodded to the cooler beneath the trees. "Sure hope there's some water in there."

"Sure. I'll get you some," Dawson volunteered. The lawyer wasn't one of the fishermen the staff was instructed to coddle, but he was a cool sort of guy, so

113

Dawson didn't mind. He bent to retrieve a bottle of chilled water to offer the attorney.

The other kayaks bumped in behind him in staggered stages. Rand Galloway and Sydney Branch floated up in green vessels, followed by the lady Sly in bright yellow. Not far behind came Kent Haney in his own green kayak.

"Guys," Walker instructed the anglers, adding a quick, "and lady. This is the one official rest stop. If anyone needs to use the facility, now is your chance."

As the group made use of the porta-potty tucked modestly away from the crossing and milled around the cooler, Dawson handed out water and fresh, crisp apples. Ryan pulled kayaks across the concrete roadway to the pooled water on the other side.

Dawson kept an eye on the kayak that was about to meet its unfortunate fate. He only half-listened to the fish reports Rand and Sydney gave, each man trying to out-lie the other. Sly laughed at their foolishness and encouraged Dawson not to believe any of it. By the time he politely listened to their tales and murmured the appropriate comeback, a pickup truck toddled across the bridge. The driver stopped to issue a friendly hello.

Leaving him to the others, Dawson hurried across the bridgeway. He could use the truck for camouflage. "Which one is it?" he hissed lowly to his friend. "I had to take my eyes off it."

"Uh, this one," Ryan said, pointing to one of the three green kayaks.

As Dawson bent to work his mischief, Ryan added in an uncertain voice, "Or maybe it was this one."

Dawson snapped upright. "Well? Which one is it?" he demanded.

"This one. Definitely this one," his friend decided, indicating his last choice.

Dawson skipped over to it and made quick work

114

of loosening the storage hatch seal and the drain plug in the bottom. "You'd better be right, dude," he hissed, "because this could get us both fired."

C⸺

At the far end of the river, Blackie deftly maneuvered his way between the three kayaks. If the anglers thought his age would slow him down and make him clumsy upon the water, they had another think coming. Blackie was born to fish, on land or water. It made him no never-mind where or how he caught the rascals, as long as he caught them.

"How old are you, anyway?" Melvin taunted. "Don't all this paddlin' make you all tuckered out?"

Blackie was undeterred by the insult. He had been listening to the man—who wasn't much more than ten years his junior, if Blackie's guess was right—all afternoon. Melvin had complained about one thing after another. They were in the wrong part of the river. There was too much water seeping into his kayak. Butch Tanger bumped into him and scared away his fish. George hummed too loud; it broke his concentration.

"That white hair growing in your ears, too?" Melvin jeered. "I asked how old you are."

"Old enough to know that there fish is too small to weigh," Blackie said without rancor. "Best throw 'im back and try for a better one."

"Who do you think you are, old man?"

Blackie didn't answer right away. He held his head at an angle, as if listening to something beyond the blowhard in the blue kayak. The more he listened, the deeper the lines furrowed upon his forehead.

"We should turn back," he announced abruptly.

"Turn back?" Butch's voice was sharp. "Is this the boundary line already?"

"Not exactly."

115

"Then why would we turn back?"

"This part of the river ain't safe," Blackie warned.

Melvin wasn't convinced. "What do you mean, it's not safe? Have you gone plumb crazy, old man? There's not a rapid in sight!" He noticed the way the older man listened intently to his surroundings. "Can't hear one, either," he insisted.

"I ain't talkin' about rapids. What's ahead is a sight far worse."

"And just what is it you see?" George Hernandez sounded as if he were humoring the older man. When he looked downriver, he saw only that the river flattened and spread over a bed of naked rocks and jagged limestone. The stream of water cutting into the rocks looked deep enough and strong enough to carry the kayaks without problem. In his estimation, the course ahead appeared more exciting than it did dangerous. The Llano was known for rapids hidden amid the treacherous rocks.

Blackie evaded a direct answer. "Just trust me on this. We don't need to go further downriver."

"We can't go upriver either, you old fool!" Melvin bellowed. "We'd have to fight the current."

"Better to fight the current, than what's ahead."

Melvin was determined to prove him wrong. With a few mighty strokes of his paddle, he pushed his kayak out in front of the others. "I ain't afraid of a few extra rocks," he claimed. "You may not have the talent to weave among them, but I do."

"I'm a'tellin' you, Melvin Maddox," Blackie said with a stubborn edge in his voice, "you don't want to go down there."

Melvin was the kind of man who loved a challenge. Blackie's unreasonable request made him all the more eager to see what danger lay ahead. "And I'm telling you I do. I think the other side of those rocks will make a dandy fishing hole. If I catch a Guad, you'll have to come and weigh it. Save your energy for paddling, old man. Don't waste it trying to stop me."

Blackie shook his shaggy white head. "Dang fool," he muttered.

"Are there rapids we can't see from here?" George asked.

"Not exactly rapids, but it can dunk your boat, all the same."

With their own kayaks drifting further downstream, they watched Melvin's determined strokes to distance himself ahead. "Melvin's a decent boater," Butch said with confidence. "He can manage a strong current, if that's your worry."

"Can't be too strong," George contended. "I can't hear a thing."

"Listen harder," Blackie instructed.

Both men cocked their heads the way he had done, straining to hear the sounds of danger. Instead, they heard the lazy lap of the river against their kayaks, interrupted by an occasional splash from the fish or the song of an overheard bird.

Hearing nothing else, George shook his head. With a shrug of disinterest, he threw out another cast.

But Butch still listened. "It almost sounds like a voice," he said, clearly surprised.

"And what's that voice sayin'?" Blackie asked, even though he already knew the answer.

"It's almost like it's saying 'Go away. We don't want you.'"

George made a noisy protest from his kayak. "That's a crock full, if ever I've heard it! Don't let this old geezer fill your head with nonsense," he warned his peer.

"You don't know about Bluffton, do you?" Blackie challenged.

He was clearly confused. "That little corner store

117

going to Lake Buchanan on 261?"

"That's the new site of the town. Before that, there was another Bluffton, but it was swallowed up by the lake. They started evacuating the town when the dam was built in '37, but it was supposed to take years for the waters to fill in. There came a flood that year, twenty-plus inches, they say, and it washed over the town before some folks had a chance to clear out. Swallowed the town up whole. Homes. Churches. Cotton gin. Hotel. Even a cemetery."

Butch's gulp was audible. "All that's under Lake Buchanan?"

"Sure 'nough," Blackie confirmed. "And on a rare occasion, when there's a severe drought and the lake sinks to meager levels, you can catch a glimpse of it again. Brings out all the lookers, you know, which riles the ghosts even more."

"Ghosts?" George's voice was sharp. He jerked his head in the older man's direction, suddenly interested in what he had to say.

"You don't reckon you can flood an entire town and not have a ghost or two lingering behind, do you?" The bent of Blackie's voice leaned toward contempt. "And some of them ghosts are downright resentful. When Roosevelt's New Deal created Buchanan Dam, folks were forced out of their homes. Most of them didn't care one wit about bringing electricity to the Hills. I 'member my old pappy talking about some of his kin, Henry and Helen York, who refused to leave their farm. Said if the lake took their home and their livelihood, it could take them, too. They fought against the dam tooth and nail, but it made no never mind in the end. Once the rains came and the waters started risin', there was no gettin' out. All that remains are their spirits, still fightin' the coming of the dam. I reckon that's them we hear, warning the politicians to stay away."

The story visibly shook Butch, but George remained skeptical. "You're full of it, old timer. We're miles from the dam."

"That's true enough," Blackie allowed, his white beard bobbing his agreement. "But they say when the waters ebb and flow, so do the spirits. It's not uncommon to find some of 'em floating along in the local rivers. The Yorks ain't the only ones left behind, you know."

"No," George snorted, "I don't know!"

"Just look up yonder, then. Why's Melvin about to capsize? Ain't no swift current. Ain't no deep eddies. Just a couple of disgruntled spirits, trying to change the course of history."

Ahead of them in the river, Melvin frantically paddled his boat, his arms flailing from one side of the tiny craft to the other. The kayak whirled at a dizzying rate, spinning for no apparent reason. But for the mad waves pushed off by his bizarre exhibition, the river around him flowed at its natural pace.

"What's happening? What's he doing?" Butch asked, his voice sharp with alarm.

"He's trying not to capsize, but it's a losin' battle."

"Shouldn't we do something?"

"What would we do? He's in no danger. The water's not deep. The current's not even that strong. He may get himself disqualified for leaving his craft, but he ain't going to drown," Blackie said with confidence.

⸺

"Yo, Judge! Over here!"

It was a familiar call of the afternoon, keeping Walker busier than he ever imagined.

As was so often the case, before he finished weighing and measuring one fish, two other fishermen called out for his services. He spent the afternoon rowing from one kayak to another. He then judiciously recorded his findings in the official logbook.

"That was a good one," Walker reported to the female angler as he released her latest fish back into the water. "Three pounds, three ounces on the dot. Nice job."

Sly slid her phone back into its waterproof pouch after documenting the catch with a photo. "Thanks. He was a nice one, all right."

Walker glanced at his watch. "Thirty more minutes, folks," he called. "Make these last catches count."

After issuing the time warning, he rowed toward Kent. The fisherman had been notorious for lagging behind the rest of the group all afternoon. By contrast, Rand was at the front of the pack, always the first to venture into new waters. Walker wondered if keeping to opposite ends was a deliberate act on both their parts. At any rate, the distance between the two made his job more difficult and provided quite the workout for the day.

Rand took the thirty-minute warning to heart and steered his vessel toward new territory. There was a section of river ahead where the banks narrowed and became more defined, characterized for once by more soil than stone. The cacti and yucca plants yielded to mesquite and cedars, and a handful of live oaks offered shade on a sultry July afternoon. The inviting vignette hinted at a pleasant ending for the highly competitive fishing session.

Sly wasn't far behind Rand, with Sydney working his way downstream to join them. Walker paddled his kayak ahead of Kent's to keep in closer contact with the others.

Instead of crowding into the narrow channel, Sydney cast his line where the river was still wide and flat. There, he caught a lively Guad worthy of weighing.

"Good work," Walker said with approval. "Three pounds, three quarter ounces."

"Now if I can just keep afloat," Sydney grinned. "I've been bailing out water for the last half hour."

Walker's brows drew together in concern. He had been alert to potential problems all afternoon, but the day had gone surprisingly well. Still, this could be an instance of sabotage.

"Why didn't you say something earlier?" he asked. "Have you—"

A surprised yelp interrupted him before he finished. He whirled around to find the source, visually locating the other anglers. He spotted Sly downriver, her arms flailing above her head as she battled an invisible enemy.

"Problems, Patterson?" Walker called, already turning his kayak around to paddle that way.

The fisherwoman didn't answer, busy batting her arms in all directions as she freed herself from her unknown assailant.

"Careful, Sly," Walker cautioned. "It could be barbed wire."

"On a river?" she asked in surprise. She had never fished the Llano, and certainly not by kayak.

"A few of the local ranchers seem to think they can claim ownership of the river. I've seen it come up in more than one case." He kept an eye on her as she fought against an empty silhouette. "Hold on, I'm headed that way," he promised.

"It's not barbed wire!" she finally answered. "I feel it, more than I see it."

"Could be a spider web," Sydney suggested.

Walker suspected it was translucent filament line, strung here as it had been on the Guadalupe. The more Sly batted at the air, and the closer her kayak bobbed toward the banks, the more the limbs above her trembled. The lines, Walker presumed, were tied among the tree limbs. Each time Sly hit or tugged a line, it set off a chain

121

reaction.

Leaves and twigs floated down upon the unsuspecting angler. The more the leaves quaked, the more that came down. Soon big, shaggy scales of Spanish moss fell from above. With the moss came the debris and the multitude of tiny creatures living among the gnarled epiphytes.

Sly yelped and jumped to her feet, almost upsetting her tiny river craft. If not for a keen sense of balance and the natural agility of an athlete, she would have upset the kayak and tumbled into the river. Instead, she swerved and swayed from inside the vessel as a litany of bugs, lizards, and frogs rained down upon her.

While the other fishermen couldn't help but laugh at the amusing sight, Walker rushed in closer. Water flew from his oars as he paddled furiously into the channel, narrowing the distance between himself and the targeted angler. If his suspicions were correct, Sly could still be in danger.

Before Walker could get a proper view of the triggering mechanism, Sly's unguided kayak bumped into the riverbank. Again, the angler seemed to surf the shifting waters from her kayak, somehow managing to retain an upright position and staying with her vessel.

A loud *crack!* stilled the air. For a split second, there was silence.

Sly's scream broke the quiet as a large oak limb fell from the sky and landed atop her, driving her back down into the kayak. It sent her sprawled backwards, legs crooked over the cockpit seat. Her head hit the stern of the kayak with a sickening thud.

Walker grabbed his two-way radio, sending out an emergency call for the second day in a row.

All hopes of ending the day on a peaceful note were shattered.

# CHAPTER 16

Hannah paced the length of her office. "We have to call it off. There's just not another way. We have to call off the tournament."

"I agree," Sadie said. "We don't have a choice."

"It's a true shame," her sister agreed. "But I agree. It's simply too dangerous to allow this tournament to continue."

Walker's solemn voice drew the women's attention when he appeared unexpectedly in the doorway. "I'm afraid it's not that simple."

"And why not?" Hannah challenged, her blue eyes ablaze. "I have the safety of the remaining contestants to think about!"

Not waiting for an invitation, Walker plopped down on the sofa. With the ease of a man totally comfortable with the room itself and its occupants, he rested his booted heels on the coffee table and released a long-suffering sigh.

Sadie disappeared long enough to return with a cold longneck bottle of his favorite beer. In her absence,

Hannah filled him in on the latest news from the hospital. Out of respect for Sadie, she didn't continue the argument without her.

"Ahmed is showing slow but encouraging progress. They hope to slowly bring him out of his medically induced coma tomorrow. Jimbo is making great progress and may be released from the hospital in the next couple of days. Sly suffered a concussion and has severe stress to the ligaments in both shins, but should be fully recovered within a few days. She was released with orders to stay off her feet, quiet and resting, for the next twenty-four hours."

"Thanks, Sadie," Walker said to the returning woman. "You have no idea how badly I need this right now."

Hannah gave him time to take one long, satisfied draw before she pelted him with questions. "What do you mean, it's not that simple? I'm sure when we tell the sponsors that there's been a string of accidents that are really no accidents at all, they'll understand our decision. The same with the contestants. When we tell them our suspicions and explain it's for their own safety, I know they'll understand. Why wouldn't they? Why do you think this will turn complicated? We have a very valid argument. If these acts are deliberate, we have no choice but to cancel."

"That's the thing. We can't prove any of them have been deliberate. As unlikely as it seems, this could be a series of very unfortunate but natural incidents."

"What about the limb that fell on Sly?" Sadie asked. "Had it been cut—"

"—or did it simply break?" With a smirk, Fred added, "At precisely the exact time Sly happened to be under it."

"Unfortunately, by the time the sheriff's office responded to the call, the limb had washed downstream,"

124

Walker reported.

"Or had been removed," suggested Hannah.

In answer, Walker tipped his bottle toward her in a mock toast before taking another swig.

"I still don't see—"

Before Hannah could continue, Walker informed her in a quiet voice, "More than one person has already threatened to sue, should we cancel the tournament."

"Who?" Fred demanded. "Who threatened to sue us?"

It warmed Hannah's heart to hear the older woman say 'us.' She knew her friends would never let her face this fiasco alone. Even if they had no financial stake in the town and its sponsored events, they had an emotional, physical, and psychological stake in it. She could depend on her dear friends to see her through whatever obstacles she faced.

The same could be said for Walker. It was more than simply the fact that he was her attorney and the executor of Wilhelmina's estate and trust. It was more than the fact that the handsome lawyer and she were romantically involved. Walker shared a history with the former owner of the town. He shared a history with Sadie and Fred. He considered it his inherent duty to take care of them still: the town, the inn, the sisters, and, yes, the new owner. It was as much a matter of heart and honor as it was duty.

That didn't mean she agreed with all his overprotective ways or all his decisions, even when rooted in best interests and legality.

"And why?" Hannah wanted to know. "How do they know we're considering it? How do they even know there was another accident?"

"It's a small community, Hannah," Walker reminded her, "and something like this is big news. And while they may not know for certain that we've discussed

125

calling off the contest, they have to know we would consider it. So just in case, they made their positions abundantly clear."

"Which is?"

He rubbed the back of his neck with his free hand. "*Luckenbach Poles* and *Johnson City Outfitters* insisted they have too much at stake to pull out now. By the end of the conversation, both suggested I speak with their lawyers before making a decision that we'll come to regret. When I reminded Walter Birch that *I* was his lawyer, he said that was apt to change."

Interspersed with her aggravation, Hannah felt a spark of empathy. "I'm sorry, Walker," she said, her voice soft.

"*Rafts to Go* didn't threaten a lawsuit, but they do want to see the tournament through. I have an unread message from *Matousek's Market*. I expect to hear something along similar lines from them, as well."

"Even if the sponsors want to proceed, the contestants may have a different opinion. They may feel it's too dangerous to continue."

"Think about what you just said, Hannah," he urged. "If these aren't accidents as we suspect, then one of those contestants is the perpetrator of the crimes. He—or she—is going to great lengths to eliminate either someone specific, or the group in general. They aren't likely to pull out now."

Hannah raked her hands through her dark tresses. "You're right, of course," she said upon a deep sigh. "They've risked too much to quit now."

"Do we have any idea who's doing this?" Sadie asked, dropping her voice to a low and urgent whisper.

In answer, Hannah went to her desk and withdrew her sheet of paper with the suspect list.

"I made a list," she explained. "I put a question mark beside a person's name for whatever motive or opportunity I felt they might have. You'll notice that six of the names have more than one question mark, making them more likely to be our suspect."

She handed the list to Walker. The sisters crowded around, looking over his shoulder as she continued, "In light of today's events, I think Gil Mendoza and Sly Patterson can be taken off the list. I give Sly enough credit not to be a victim of her own devious plan. And with a second wave of 'accidents,' it lets Gil off the hook. He no longer has anything to gain by eliminating the competition."

"Agreed." Walker studied the paper for a moment. "Good detective work, Hannah."

His warm smile made her feel ridiculously pleased with herself. "Thanks," she murmured.

"What earned George the additional mark?"

"I overheard a conversation inside his and Ahmed's room that first night. I can't be certain, but I think it was George speaking. He was very angry with one of the other fishermen, insisting he had to be stopped."

"Who was he talking about?" Sadie asked.

"I don't know. Somebody he thought was messing with people's heads and hearts, not to mention their pocketbooks." A memory surfaced, and Hannah's eyes widened.

Seeing her expression, Fred asked in a sharp voice, "What? What are you thinking?"

"I couldn't hear what the other man, presumably Ahmed, said, but when he apparently didn't agree, George got angry with him, too. He called him a coward for not standing up to the bully. You don't think... You don't think he may have been angry enough to harm Ahmed, do you?"

While Sadie and Fred made sounds of surprise, Walker remained a voice of reason. "There's no way he— or anyone else, for that matter—could have known for certain that Ahmed would be the one to find the snake's nest."

"You're right, of course. I just know that he was very angry. And after that altercation I saw at the fish fry, I assumed he was referring to Rand. Coupled with other remarks he's made, I felt it was worthy of two marks."

"I'm not disputing you," Walker was quick to say. "I happen to agree. Before the ambulance even arrived for Sly, George expressed his concerns that the tournament might be canceled. He threatened to sue if we called it off."

"Wait. Back up," Fred said. "What altercation at the fish fry?"

"I saw two men arguing with Rand. I don't remember the exact words, but I think they accused him of something underhanded. Not exactly cheating, but maybe manipulating things his way. It got pretty intense."

"Who were the men?"

"At the time, I had no idea. Now I think it could have been Gil Mendoza or possibly Butch Tanger. I think the other man was probably Sydney."

Sadie wiggled her fingers toward Walker. "Put another question mark by Sydney," she advised.

Walker looked back at the list. "Billy Joe?"

"I guess he seems a bit… desperate, for lack of a better word. He's made a few cracks about giving him special treatment because of his age. The second mark is because he's from the general area and could, hypothetically, have better access to rigging the fishing holes."

"*If* he knew where we were fishing," Sadie pointed out.

"The thought was that he was more likely to have local contacts. And with today being even closer to his hometown…"

Fred thought she had a more likely suspect. "Sydney Branch is originally from Llano," she said. "It makes sense that he would have contacts in the area. A friend or relative who knows the river—"

"—or even owns the land where the accident took place—" her sister put in.

"—who could help him carry out his nefarious deed. Thankfully, Sly wasn't seriously injured, but she could have been. This could have turned out so much worse than it did."

"Absolutely," Walker agreed. "But there's still the point that he, too, would have to know where we were fishing in order to rig it."

A frown dipped the edges of Hannah's mouth. "So, we're back to the possibility we discussed the other night." For the benefit of the sisters, she said, "We have a leak."

"A leak? Who?" squeaked Sadie.

"I have no idea. I want to believe it's innocent. The first time, Walker convinced me it could have been an innocent mistake. Something someone overheard. A landowner at one of the locations may have made a casual comment, and the wrong person heard it. But after to-day…"

Walker nodded in agreement, his tone solemn. "I think it's obvious someone has been leaking information."

"Who would do such a thing? We've been so care-ful!" Fred insisted. "Sister and I know the ropes. We don't reveal a single detail until it's absolutely necessary."

"We know that," Hannah said hastily. "Walker and I aren't accusing you of anything."

"I didn't think you were. I was thinking about when it becomes necessary." Her eyes narrowed in thought. "The evening before the Guadalupe trip, we prepped for breakfast. Sadie, who was—"

Without waiting for the rest of the question, Sadie answered with, "Carrie, Gusto, and Brianna."

"But I'm fairly certain we didn't mention where

we were going, just that we would serve breakfast en route."

"On the other hand," Sadie added, "it was necessary to tell the kids who helped today. Some of them are underage, so we felt it prudent to alert their parents of travel plans. We stressed the importance of confidentiality—"

"—but who knows if they heeded our warnings?"

"There's always the possibility the leak came from one of our sponsors," Hannah reasoned. "Quite by accident, I'm sure, but a leak, nonetheless."

Rubbing his neck, Walker thought aloud, "Theoretically, any of the contestants could have come across the confidential information. To carry out their plans, they had to have an accomplice. Someone local to the area."

Hannah picked up the thought. "And even though they could, in theory, hire a stranger..."

"It stands to reason they would go with someone they trusted."

Sadie and Fred nodded in agreement. "Which brings us back to our local boys, Billy Joe and Sydney."

"There goes Sydney's name again, popping up," mumbled Hannah.

"Which is a shame." Fred's voice sounded sorrowful. "He's a talented young man. And doing very well in the standings. Conceivably, he could win the championship."

"We don't know for certain he's the guilty party," the lawyer among them said swiftly. "A man is innocent until proved guilty."

"And that brings us back to our original problem. We don't have the luxury of waiting to prove guilt or innocence. We need to call off this tournament. Now." Hannah's voice was adamant.

"Again, it's not that easy. You could face multiple lawsuits."

130

"Isn't there a term for things like this? Something that's beyond our control and allows us to cancel for the safety of the contestants?"

"*Force majeure*," Walker supplied. "I'm not sure it applies in this case. At any rate, they can still sue. Whether or not they can win is up to the judge, or possibly a jury."

"But if their lives are in danger...!" Hannah protested.

"We can't prove that's the case. At this point, both the Comal County and the Llano County sheriff's departments still maintain there isn't enough evidence to make this an active case. Which definitely weakens our stance on canceling the event."

"Then, what do we do?" Sadie wanted to know.

Walker turned toward Hannah as he answered. "I think our only option is to continue with the contest, with one caveat. I think we should push the final event to Friday morning, rather than tomorrow evening. That will allow Sly a full twenty-four hours to rest, per doctor's orders."

"Did she make the final four?" Hannah asked.

"We haven't officially certified the results, but yes."

"I don't like it," Hannah said, just to make her position clear. "But if everyone agrees that's the best thing to do, I suppose I'll go along with it."

"Given that neither sheriff's department can't find any hard evidence—"

"—and given that both the sponsors *and* the contestants might sue—"

"—we think it's best to announce the four finalists and let them decide whether or not they want to proceed," Fred replied.

Hannah couldn't help the frown puckering her forehead. It wasn't that she disagreed. She simply didn't understand the sisters' uncanny ability to read the other's thoughts so well.

"You said 'we' without even asking Sadie," she pointed out. "How do you know she feels the same way?"

Fred turned to her sister. "Am I wrong?"

"Of course not. That's exactly how I feel."

Fred turned back with an *'I told you so'* expression on her face.

"I don't know why I even asked," Hannah muttered. "You two have some weird psychic connection."

"Thank you for not saying we share a brain, like some people are apt to do. We prefer to think of it as a superpower, magnified by two," Sadie preened.

Hannah relented with a sigh. "I suppose I'm outnumbered. I guess the contest will go on as planned. We can announce the winners and the delay at breakfast, and then meet with the finalists in private."

"Will Sly need to be in attendance, or can we discuss it with her separately?" Sadie wanted to know.

"Given the circumstances, I don't expect her to attend breakfast. Thank you, by the way, for offering to let her stay at the cabin with you."

"She's in no shape to climb these stairs!" Sadie said.

"And she can use a bit of peace and quiet, not to mention a bit of pampering. She's more than welcome to stay at our place." With a wink, Fred added, "We gals have to stick together, you know."

# CHAPTER 17

Before the sun fully hung in the sky, Hannah trekked out to the barn to milk Buttercrunch.

If someone had told her six months ago that she would be acquainted with a bovine—let alone that she would milk one, and gladly so—Hannah would have thought them insane. At the time, her life was in Houston. She was an investment analyst with a well-established investment firm. Her life revolved around fifty-hour work weeks, board meetings, mandatory dinner parties, and charts and graphs. She adored lists. Everything in her life was orderly and efficient, and surrounded by concrete and skyscrapers.

It had all come crashing down like a house made of cards.

More precisely, it came down like a house built on embezzled funds. When the government seized the firm where she had worked and froze her investment and retirement accounts, her world as she knew it ended. She was left without a job, without a career, and with no prospects for future employment.

It was then, and only then, that she remembered her birthday gift, four months prior. Because she had nothing better to do, she had come to the Texas Hill Country to investigate.

*And the rest*, as the saying went, *was history*.

Something about this aging stagecoach inn had struck a chord in her. Chalk it up to her vulnerability at the moment, but she pulled one long, deep breath of the country air into her lungs, and she was hooked. A peace-fulness settled into her bones, and she had the achingly beautiful but unfamiliar sense of belonging.

Now here she was, living a life she never imaged for herself. A life she never knew she needed, but one she already appreciated.

"Hello, girl," she cooed to the gentle giant. "I've come to relieve you."

She settled onto the stool, placing the bucket be-neath the cow's swollen udder. She rubbed her hands to warm them, recalling the lesson Walker taught her the first time she milked a cow. *How would you like cold hands on your... on you?* he had asked. She could laugh about it now, and the argument that ensued over her actu-ally touching a cow.

In just a few short months, the routine now came naturally to Hannah. She even looked forward to the rhythmic tug and squeeze, and the steady squirt of milk against metal. She found it was a peaceful start to her day.

Something told her that, today, she would need to take peace wherever she could find it.

She wondered how the finalists would take the news. Would they be concerned over their safety? Had it already occurred to them that they could be in danger? Or was the thought of winning ten thousand dollars and a claim to fame worth the risk? It didn't help that local law enforcement negated concerns of serious risk.

How would the spectators take the news? Their

new plan meant the final phase wouldn't take place until a day later. Some of the fans—perhaps even some of the final four—hadn't planned to stay an additional night. Sadie assured Hannah she would take care of reservation concerns, but there would undoubtedly be some who complained about the delay. She imagined Melvin Maddox and Bart Hinkle would be the first to do so, not to mention be the most vocal of the lot.

Done with the milking, Hannah thanked the contributor, unharnessed her so she could roam about the pen, and carried the morning's reward from the barn. As she walked back toward the inn, she realized she wasn't the only one to do so.

Despite the early hour, Tallia entered the front door of the inn. Hannah could almost convince herself the long-legged woman had been out for an early morning run. Almost. But no one ran in high heels, particularly with straps so dainty. It was more likely that she had been out all night and was just returning to her husband's room.

So much had happened over the last four days, Hannah had given little thought to the woman, other than to disparage her skimpy outfits. Now, however, Hannah wondered about the bruise from the first night. Who had inflicted the damage to Tallia's cheek? Did it have anything to do with the unexplained 'accidents' that kept occurring?

Unless the accidents were aimed at one particular person, Hannah could hardly see how the two events might be related. Jimbo, Ahmed, and Sly were the unfortunate recipients of the acts. Hannah couldn't recall having seen any interaction between the tall redhead and the three injured parties.

Even if Kent Haney was the jealous type—and he didn't appear to be so—the most likely targets for any warped sense of revenge on his part would be Rand and

Sydney, but neither man had been involved in the accidents.

Not only that, but so far, Sydney was their prime suspect.

Deciding Tallia's sordid love life was none of her concern, Hannah watched the woman disappear into the inn. She would see her again soon enough, she was sure.

C

"Good morning, everyone!" Hannah greeted the breakfast crowd an hour or so later. "We have some good news to share with you this morning. The doctors say Ahmed is showing marked improvement. Jimbo is expected to be released from the hospital tomorrow. And Sly reports to having a good night and feeling halfway human this morning. So, we can all feel encouraged and know our prayers are working. Please, don't stop now. They all have a way to go before being one hundred percent, but I feel confident they'll be back among us soon."

She was sandwiched between Sadie and Fred. Together, the three of them were a formidable force. Having their support gave Hannah the confidence to continue her speech.

"We have some other news to share with you this morning. D—"

"Yeah, like who the final four are!" Bart Hinkle called out, interrupting her.

"And we will get to that, just as soon as we can. First, we need to inform you of a change in schedule. Due to yesterday's turn of events, we have chosen to postpone the final phase of the tournament, originally scheduled for late this afternoon. Instead—"

Again, she was interrupted. This time, several spoke up, expressing their displeasure. Most thought the tournament was being postponed indefinitely, a fact they were adamantly opposed to.

Fred took the mic and gave it a series of sharp, re-petitive taps. It was enough to get their attention and quieten the crowd. "Settle down!" she called. "And hush up! You don't even know what we're proposing, and you're already complaining. Two of you are threatening lawsuits. Just hush, all of you!" She handed the mic back to Hannah with a serene smile. "You may proceed."

"As I was saying, we will hold the final round to-morrow morning at nine o'clock. I hope this doesn't pose too big of an inconvenience for you, but the matter has been decided and is not up for discussion. If you have concerns about your reservation, see Sadie after breakfast, and she'll get you taken care of. Naturally, there will be no charge for the additional night's stay. If you need ideas of what to do in the area since you now have a free day, drop by the front desk and ask for some brochures." She pointedly ignored the people trying to ask questions. "I know we're all anxious to hear the outcome of yester-day's competition. Without further ado, I present two of our esteemed tournament judges, Walker Jacoby and Robert Lee McNutt, to make that announcement. Please give these gentleman a round of applause."

As a politician accustomed to making speeches, County Judge McNutt spoke to the restless crowd at length, drawing out the announcement they were anxious to hear. He told a fish story that was only mildly amusing, thanked all the sponsors once again, and launched into a detailed explanation of how they judged this phase of the contest.

Hannah tuned him out as she searched the room for anyone seeming to carry a guilty conscience. Most looked more aggravated than apologetic. While they wait-ed to hear their fate, the politician droned on in a self-serving speech. Others looked slightly bored. They knew they weren't among the final contestants. Not a single person had 'guilty' written across his or her forehead. Not even Tallia, who wore another of her barely decent out-fits.

It was the same outfit she had on earlier this morn-ing, if Hannah weren't mistaken. Upon closer inspection, it looked neither wrinkled nor dirty, making Hannah wonder if she had actually worn it the night before. But if she weren't sneaking back into the inn after being out all night, then what had she been doing out so early? She had come from the direction of the RV pads. The same pads where Rand's RV was parked.

Quite without realizing it, Hannah stood before the crowd with a distinct frown on her face, just as the bag weights from the day before were finally announced.

Fred nudged her, hissing from the side of her mouth, "Smile. You're supposed to look happy."

Hannah gulped and stretched her lips into a big smile. She clapped along with everyone else as the judges congratulated all the anglers and named the four finalists.

"That means, ladies and gentlemen, that we have our final four who will compete in tomorrow morning's competition," Judge McNutt said. He used a hushed and somber game-show-host voice to build excitement. He might have been confirming the final answer prior to be-coming a millionaire. "Mr. Jacoby, just to be clear, will you give us those names?"

"It is my honor and great pleasure to announce our finalists. Contestants, please stand as I call your name, so we can recognize you and your impressive accomplish-ments. Rand Galloway." He waited for the applause to die down before calling, "Kent Haney."

Tallia screeched with excitement, throwing her arms around her husband's neck and wiggling with glee. She insisted on taking her place by his side as he stood.

"Sydney Branch." The crowd clapped a third time and called out words of encouragement, but most eyes were on Tallia. She bounced in excitement, defying the laws of gravity as her tank top stretched and strained to cover her bobbing breasts. She remained at her husband's side, but her enthusiasm could have been for any of the three men standing.

"And, even though she can't join us right now, Sly Patterson." When the applause died down, Walker continued, "We need you three gentlemen to stay for a special briefing immediately following this. Before we dismiss, however, I want to go on record as saying how challenging it was to make the distinction between who moved forward and who had to be eliminated. This was by far the closest competition I have had the honor of judging. All of you should be commended for your fishing skills and your participation in this year's Trifishlon. Let's give a huge round of applause for all of our contestants!"

With his upbeat speech, breakfast ended on a positive note. Soon, the crowd dissipated and the finalists, sans Sly, moved into the inner office for a private discussion.

Hannah and her team laid out the situation as they saw it.

"This year's tournament has seen more than its fair share of... unusual occurrences. We've been in close contact with the sheriff's offices and are investigating each incident. While there's no direct evidence that these are anything other than random and unfortunate accidents, there is obviously an increased danger in going forward with the final phase of the contest. Anticipating additional problems seems to be par for the course this year. With that in mind, this is your opportunity to excuse yourself from the competition."

"And forfeit the chance to win?" Kent Haney scoffed. "No, thank you."

"I agree. I haven't come this far to roll over and play dead now," Sydney blustered.

139

"Same here," Rand said, but his tone was more subdued. After a slight hesitation, he added, "This isn't the first time I've had a target on me. I'm used to keeping one eye on my back."

"We'll do everything in our power to keep you safe. At any point you feel uncomfortable, don't hesitate to speak up. We'll have additional personnel on hand for tomorrow's competition. At the first sign of danger, we'll do whatever it takes to shut it down, even if it means calling a halt to the competition."

Sydney spoke for all of them. "Like we said, we aren't pulling out now."

After covering a few more details, the meeting broke up, and Hannah walked the judges to their vehicles. She lingered in the morning sunshine, enjoying the day before it turned uncomfortably hot.

A group of children played a game of dodgeball in the town green. She wasn't surprised to see Orlan Valera in the midst of them, jumping and swerving with every strategically thrown ball. He danced happily in the front line, daring the ball to pass through his ghostly presence. The apparition did a fair job of dodging its path, even when his efforts knocked the battered wide-brimmed hat from his head.

Once, as he swooped to retrieve it, he caught sight of Hannah watching him with an amused smile on her face. Ever the gentleman, he promptly bowed in respect. The ball careened through his head in a straight shot, but he never flinched.

Hannah crooked a finger to beckon him her way. Since she didn't know how to summon him directly, today's game of dodgeball offered an opportunity to speak to the vaquero ghost.

"Hello, *senorita*," he greeted.

She glanced around to make certain no one saw or heard her talking to thin air. "Hello to you, Mr. Valera. I see you're enjoying yourself with the children." She had discovered his fondness for children during their opening weekend. More surprising had been the fact that, on occasion, some of the children could see and interact with him.

"It keeps a body young, *si?*"

Hannah couldn't very well dispute him. One hundred and forty-odd years later, he still looked like a young man.

"I may need your help," she said, instead.

He didn't hesitate. "Absolutely."

Hannah moved closer, so that her words didn't carry. "Tomorrow morning, we'll be fishing at the creek. Can you be there?"

"It will be my pleasure. What can I do? Do you need a waterspout?" He spun his wispy body, faster and faster, moving away from her in a dizzying spiral. The dirt beneath his feet rose, stirring and spinning into a small dust devil. He spun playfully toward the children, making them scatter amid squeals of delight, before stilling and appearing in front of her once again. "Do you wish for the fish to jump out of the water and onto the banks? Or for them to swim far, far downstream?"

Not needing anything so drastic, Hannah shook her head. "I need you to keep an eye on our contestants. I think one or more of them may be in danger. I need you to watch them closely and keep them safe."

"I am honored to help, *senorita.*"

"Thank you." It felt strange, asking for help from a ghost, but Orlan Valera had proved himself useful on several occasions. "If you see anything suspicious, please let me know."

Before she could ask anything further, she heard her name called. "Miss Duncan! Miss Duncan, I must speak to you. Right now!"

Hannah was less than thrilled to see Melvin Maddox hurrying toward her. She glanced toward the inn, judging how quickly she could make an escape. Realizing she was stuck, she offered him a small smile. "I have a moment or two. How may I help you, Mr. Maddox?"

"It's about the way I was treated yesterday! That old fool of a judge disqualified me because my kayak flipped over. What was I supposed to do? Drown?"

"I'm sorry, Mr. Maddox. The rules are very clear. All decisions by the judges are final. I cannot and will not overturn their calls. If Mr. Cole said you were disqualified, you were disqualified."

"That's malarkey, and you know it! The waters started stirring and capsized my kayak. I didn't leave my boat voluntarily. I had no choice!" He continued to rant, but his words were stolen by a sudden wind stirring behind him.

Once again, the old vaquero spun himself into a dust devil. The spiral hovered just behind the fisherman, throwing bits of sand and grit against his back. High on his soap box, Melvin Maddox was too riled to even notice. He wagged his finger in the air to make his point, his voice rising in anger.

The spirited dust devil inched closer, playing with the tail of his shirt. Caught up in his tirade, Melvin used his free hand to yank at the material, without ever missing a cross word.

Orlan spun faster. Hannah took a quick step backward, sensing he had more planned for the disrespectful fisherman.

Melvin's eyes widened into huge orbs as the whirlwind spun outward and then came in closer, pushing between the two of them. Hannah wisely jumped out of the way, but Melvin was caught in the vortex of the spinning ghost. Orlan circled him, spiraling round and round at a dizzying speed, trapping the fisherman within a freakish whirlwind that spun only for him.

Melvin cried out in alarm, but Hannah found it

difficult not to laugh. His shirt bunched and pulled against him, caught in the fierce winds. One button popped loose, followed by another. He tried spinning with the wind to keep ahead of its force, but it was a losing battle. His eyes filled with tears, perhaps from the biting grit, perhaps from the sting of terror.

By the time the shirt ripped from his body, he would have fallen helplessly to the ground, but the force of the wind kept him upright, steering him away from Hannah.

The last she saw, the whirlwind chased the shirt-less man back to his cabin.

# CHAPTER 18

He was back!

Danika pretended not to notice, even as her blood hummed with pleasure. He had slipped in behind another customer, but she knew he was there, all the same. Her senses heightened, tingling with his nearness. She felt his eyes upon her, even before she turned to catch her reflection in his polarized sunglasses.

She finished helping her customer, but she angled her body so that her best assets were on display. The old man she waited on was too nearsighted to see anything beyond his nose, but she guessed the man in the plaid shirt had excellent eyesight. Silhouetted against the window, he wouldn't need x-ray vision to see her au natural through the tee's thin material.

If her mother had been working today, she would have never gotten out of the house without a bra. But her mother had a doctor's appointment this morning and plans for shopping this afternoon. That meant her father would be far too busy covering both positions today to pay her any attention. Just to be safe, however, she had slipped a second shirt over the tee. Worn open, it was easy to tug closed when her father or co-worker was around, or to flick open, just enough to offer a glimpse of what laid beneath, when a cute guy came in.

But as the clock ticked past one, and she hoped *he* would come in, Danika chucked the over-shirt behind the register and threw caution to the wind. She reasoned that when she went away to college in just two short months, she could dress in anything she wanted.

The old man finally made his selection and was out the door. Danika fluffed her hair and sauntered toward the back of the store, where she knew that *he* waited for her. She put extra swagger into her hips and was rewarded with a big smile.

"Busy day?" he drawled.

She shrugged, nonchalantly tucking her hands into her back pockets. "A girl's gotta do what a girl's gotta do."

He appreciated the meager effort. Tallia often used the same pose. It was a pale comparison, but he wouldn't insult her by not looking. But the clock was ticking, and he didn't have time to indulge her girlish fantasies.

"And you work on commission, right?"

"Sure do." Her smile brightened. "What can I interest you in today?"

It was on the tip of his tongue to chide her on her foolishness. He was a grown man. She was just a kid. If he had been interested in what she so recklessly offered, she could be in for a world of hurt. If he was a different kind of guy, she could be putting herself in a dangerous situation. But to tell her that would put her on the offensive. She would be humiliated, and he would never be able to coax the information from her that he needed.

He couldn't encourage her foolhardy overture, and he couldn't rebuff her. But he could pretend to misunderstand. He grabbed a nearby fish-finder graph and tried to

145

sound sincere when he asked, "I'd like to know more about how this works. What can you tell me?"

She was obviously disappointed, but she nonetheless answered his questions. It didn't hurt that the graph had a hefty price tag and would earn her a nice hunk of change in commission.

With the tension eased and Danika no longer trying to seduce him, he slipped in the purpose of today's visit.

"Hey, I totally missed that tournament you told me about. I got busy fishing, and it totally slipped my mind. I really wanted to go, too. I'm bummed that I missed the whole thing."

"Actually, it's not over yet."

He tried to look surprised. "Really? I figured it was all done by now and some lucky son of a gun was ten grand richer."

"Not yet. There were a couple of random accidents, and the organizers decided to postpone it by a day. The final phase is tomorrow morning."

"Oh yeah?" He pretended preoccupation with the item in his hand. "What kind of accidents?"

"Totally random things. One guy was bitten by snakes. Another guy got tangled up in his riggings. A third guy had a limb fall on him and gave him a concussion. Things that would never happen in a single summer, yet somehow happened all in one tournament." Danika rolled her eyes to express her opinion on life's many curve balls. "Like I said. Random."

He bit back the urge to correct her. Jimbo hadn't gotten tangled in his own riggings. Those had been carefully and expertly staged, thank you very much. And Sly was hardly a *guy*. This girl needed to get her details straight, especially since he staked his entire future on the leads she gave him.

"Bummer," he said instead. "Guess it's just as

well I didn't watch any of it. What's tomorrow's torture? A river of sharks?"

"Luckily, it's not a river, at all."

She played into his hands, just as he had hoped. "Good idea. A lake offers a much larger playing field." His mouth suddenly twisted in mock horror. "But just think of the things that could go wrong, out on the wide-open water."

"Not a lake, either" Danika informed him.

He looked at her with a skeptical expression, the same one that had worked in the past. "What else is there, Miss Hot Shot, if it's not a lake and it's not a river? Don't tell me they're fishing from a swimming pool."

"There's also the creeks and streams," she reminded him smartly. "A few around here are even deep enough to hold decent fish."

"I don't believe you. The only streams I've seen here so far are more like trickles. Where you gonna find a creek deep enough to fish?" he scoffed.

Danika matched his sardonic tone. "Maybe right out the inn's front door?"

The news surprised him. He had never considered South Grape Creek as a possibility, but it made sense.

Now that he knew the final location, he had work to do. He shoved the fish finder back on the shelf and looked down at his watch. "Man, would you look at the time! I've gotta go."

The girl pouted prettily. "But you haven't been here that long."

"Yeah, but I really have to go."

He already moved away. If he left now, she might not get another chance. Twirling a lock of her hair around her finger, Danika made a bold offer. "I get off at five. I can take you to some of the best fishing holes around, if you're interested." She held her breath. They both knew she was asking about more than fishing.

147

It was time to end this. The girl had proved to be a great source of information, but now that he had the last piece of the puzzle, she was no longer of use to him. It was best to rip the bandage off and be done with it.

"The thing is, my father-in-law's waiting on me. We've got plans this evening."

"Your... father-in-law?" Her voice came out faint. With her next words, it found volume. "You're—You're *married?*" The last came out almost in a screech. "You said you had an *ex*, not a wife!"

"It's... complicated," he said. "But, hey, if I don't make it back in, you've been a terrific salesperson. Tell your boss I said so. He should give you a bonus, or at least a special sticker or something."

Her mouth worked in silent rage, reminding him of a fish. For a minute there, he worried she might cry. He hated it when girls cried, especially Tallia; for all her physical attributes, she was one ugly crier. So, he used a trick he had learned long ago. Make a woman mad enough, and her tears would evaporate into red hot anger. His reference now to a child's sticker had done the trick, drying Danika's tears right up.

Before she threw something, he flashed a parting smile and hurried out the door.

# CHAPTER 19

The final four contestants assembled on the banks of South Grape Creek, poised for the third and final round of the Trifishlon. In three short hours, one of them would be ten thousand dollars richer.

By then, they might also know the person responsible for sabotaging the tournament. The Llano County Sheriff Department had called early this morning with good news. Someone remembered seeing two local men along the section of the river where Sly was hurt, carrying a chain saw and a ladder. As both men were known for their frequent visits to jail, it hadn't taken long for the sheriff to round them up and bring them in for questioning. They admitted to cutting and rigging the limb to fall when the line was disturbed. They didn't know the name of the guy who hired them, but they could identify him on sight.

Even though it invited more drama, the best time to catch all contestants together was during the awards presentation. Once the winners were named, the entire group would scatter like seeds in the wind.

Hannah's nerves were fraught with worry and she didn't trust herself to speak coherently, so she asked Fred to address the finalists that morning. Not only did Fred have a better understanding of the process but, as one of the event's founders, she had a deep connection to the twenty-three-year-old tradition. Plus, Fred loved being in the spotlight.

The dainty woman pranced along the creek bank, dressed in one of her signature Western outfits. Because it was July in Texas and already in the high eighties at nine o'clock in the morning, she dressed accordingly. Her pressed jeans were white, and her custom-made Western shirt was the palest of blue, with white piping accents and no sleeves. A white straw hat perched atop her gray curls, coordinating with the white cowboy boots on her feet.

"As you well know," Fred sang out in her lilting voice, "the concept behind our Trifishlon is to embrace the true art of fishing. We try to emphasize the natural beauty of the sport, and the importance of being attuned to nature and our surroundings. Since the dawn of time, fishing has been a fundamental part of basic survival. True fishing isn't about fancy riggings and tricked-out poles. It's not about the latest artificial bait or technologically advanced lures. When it comes down to it, it's about understanding your prey and their natural habitat. It's about outsmarting the fish.

"So for this, our final challenge of the Hannah Trifishlon, we're going back to the basics. It will just be you, the fish, and your fishing pole. And what better way to do that than with an old-fashioned cane fishing pole? *Luckenbach Poles* was kind enough to supply each of you with the retro-styled Calcutta '55 bamboo pole and a bucket of live bait."

Murmurs moved through the crowd. Some bore the sound of approval, some of disdain. Fred ignored them all.

"These are the rules, so listen carefully. Only the bait supplied to you is allowed. You may elect to use a bobber, fish on the bottom, or a combination of both. Stringing and technique is up to you but using anything other than the supplies you are given will be grounds for disqualification. You may move along the creek at will, as long as you stay within the boundaries of Hannah. If you reach a barbed wire fence, you've reached the boundary line. Also, you must remain within sight of an official judge.

"There is a three-hour time limit. You are allowed to weigh any ten fish of your choosing, but they must be alive. If you catch a good fish, you may bring it here to the official weigh station at any time and have it recorded as one of your ten. Just know, however, that once a fish is weighed, it's official. You can also choose to keep the fish on a stringer, but remember that if it dies, it doesn't count. The tournament is officially over at noon. The fisherman with the heaviest bag will be named the official champion of this year's Hannah Trifishlon and will be awarded the grand prize."

Hannah asked some of the summer help to distribute equipment among the contestants. After Dawson and Ryan handed out poles and bait, Brianna and Carrie gave each contestant bottled water and a bag of trail mix. With their bosses watching, there was no time for Brianna to flirt or for Dawson to sabotage.

Kent was the first to get his rigging, so he grabbed it and headed upstream. He had noticed a nice little pool of water near the entrance to the property. He would start there and work his way down.

"Wait, baby!" Tallia called, breaking free of the throng of onlookers. She picked her way through the rough terrain, her long legs unsteady in the four-inch heels amid rocks and spiky grasses. Her cut-off blue jean shorts weren't long enough to hide the white of the inner pockets. When she threw her arms around her husband's neck, they did little to conceal the swell of her butt cheeks, either.

"Make me a millionaire, baby," she said, pressing her scantily clad bosom against his chest.

He didn't bother correcting her. Ten grand was a long way from a million, but Tallia had never been very good at math. She was excellent at *figures*, however, and he still liked the feel of her figure against his, even if their marriage had its fair share of troubles.

"This'll be for you, Tallia, baby," he said, pressing a kiss against her lips.

She turned away from her husband and almost bumped into Rand Galloway. With a shrug, she threw her arms around him, too.

"Best of luck to you!" She kept the words light and bright, just like her hug.

As the first two fishermen crossed the narrow footbridge to their side of the creek, Sly followed behind. She was moving slowly today, the ligaments on both shins still strained and painful. There was a large bandage beneath the floppy brim of her fishing hat, and she wore glasses to conceal the dark circles beneath her eyes and the fact that her pupils couldn't quite focus. But she had come this far, and the championship was within reach. She wasn't about to let a little thing like a concussion and pulled ligaments stop her now.

Simply seeing *one* of the frizzy-haired gargantuan in short shorts was bad enough; two was downright scary. She didn't realize she walked directly into Tallia's path until it was too late.

The two women did the awkward dance of occupying the same space. Each moved aside to allow the other past, but their timing was off. They found themselves face to face on the sideline. Tallia immediately stepped to her left, as Sly moved right. Once again, they were in each other's space.

"What? No good luck hug for me?" Sly asked with a smirk.

To her surprise, the other woman mumbled, "Ah, what the hell," and threw her arms around her, too. There was a smattering of laughter from the crowd as Sly frowned and moved across the bridge, going as quickly as her pulled muscles would allow.

It made hugging Sydney less conspicuous. As the last of the finalists collected his gear and turned toward the creek, Tallia was still in the path leading to the bridge. Sydney saw the crooked smile twisting her angular face and had just enough time to brace himself for the hug he knew was coming. She hurled her body against his and clasped both arms around his neck, pressing close.

"Good luck to you, too!" she gushed. The cheery tone was for the crowd. The extra little wiggle was just for him.

Sydney appreciated the wiggle. He especially liked the press of her warm, willing body against his; it seemed to wake things up. Despite the importance of the day and the excitement that came with it, he felt lethargic this morning. He had been awake half the night with muscle spasms in his chest and abdomen, and now his entire upper body ached. He wasn't sure, but he thought he might have a fever. His head definitely hurt, but Tallia's body hug was just the thing he needed.

*It hadn't gone unappreciated last night, either*, he thought with a chuckle. When she had cozied up to him and all but crawled inside his shirt with him, his entire body had been abuzz. When she whispered sweet promises in his ear, it was like pins and needles pricked his entire body. And when she went so far as to *bite* his earlobe, he could have sworn he felt her teeth sink into the flesh between his shoulder blades. He went weak in the knee, just thinking about it now. He had known a lot of women in his time, but none had ever had him under her spell the way Tallia did. He knew she rightfully belonged to Kent, but one day…

Sydney slung the thought from his mind, trying to focus on the task at hand. Winning ten grand would go a long way toward impressing her. Even if he could lure her away from Kent, he didn't make the kind of money needed to win Tallia's heart and keep her in the lifestyle she was accustomed to. She wore those high-dollar shoes and that fancy perfume. There wasn't much material used in her outfits, but that level of sexy didn't come cheap. If he had any hopes of winning her affections, he had to win this tournament first.

As the finalists moved into position along the banks, Sadie instructed the spectators of the rules and limitations as applied to them. They were to stay on the south side of the creek at all times, facing the fishermen. For their enjoyment, two food trucks and a shaded eating area were available.

The first half hour of fishing was slow. Only a few crappies were biting. Minnows and perch stole most of the bait, and it took the anglers a few tries to find their rhythm. For most of them, it had been years since they had fished with a simple cane pole. After the fancy mechanisms of thousand-dollar reels and aerodynamic rods, fishing with a simple bamboo pole and a length of string was foreign to them.

Rand was the first to bring a fish in to weigh. A nice largemouth bass topped the scale at three pounds and counted as his first official catch.

Because of her physical limitations, Sly chose to keep her fish on a stringer and take her chances at keeping them alive. Unless she caught something too big not to risk, she was limiting her steps. She even found a sweet little honey hole and settled in beneath the sheltering arms of a live oak. As long as the fish were biting, she wasn't budging.

From the other side of the banks, the onlookers called out words of encouragement and took bets on who would win. Rand was the crowd favorite, followed by Sydney. Kent and Sly tied for a distant third.

Brianna was thoroughly disenchanted and lost all interest in the stupid contest. She hadn't missed the way *he* smiled when that red-haired Amazon threw herself at him. After last night's no show, the teen harbored no illusions that he was truly interested in her. He had probably been using her to get information, but she had outsmarted him. She hadn't revealed a single secret.

The older man had been a nice little distraction from the silly boys she found herself surrounded by, but at least when Dawson promised to do something, he kept his word. Right then, Brianna decided she had had enough of the fishermen and their preoccupation with a bobbing cork. At least Dawson was interested, which was more than she could say for *him*.

She looked around for her co-worker but didn't see him among the crowd. He had probably gone back to the inn. Considering it was getting hotter out here by the minute, it didn't sound like a bad idea. Without as much as a glance over her shoulder, Brianna turned her back on the fickle fisherman and went in search of a sure thing.

By eleven, Sydney's upper abdomen was killing him. He felt hot and cold, all at one time. How could he be freezing, yet be sweating like he was in a sauna? It was getting increasingly difficult to breathe, too.

He stayed on the banks fishing, determined to catch the fish that kept stealing his bait. He had gotten a glimpse of the thief and knew it was a decent-sized catfish, the best he had seen so far. He was going to snag that sucker if it was the last thing he did.

Ten minutes later, his cork went under. The tug was strong enough—or perhaps, he was weak enough—

155

that the sudden movement almost ripped the bamboo from his hand. He jerked his pole to set the hook, then began the tedious process of tugging and pulling, leading the fish toward the bank. A cramp hit him as he inched the pole backwards. The fish swinging on the other end almost got away, but long minutes later, Sydney managed to land him.

The process exhausted him far more than it should have. By now, Sydney knew he was in trouble. He was having some sort of respiratory distress. An attack of some kind. If not heart, then kidney. Gallstone. Something that caused this wave of nausea and these ungodly chills racking his body. He was weak and feverish, but he was taking that fish to the weigh-in station.

"Looks like a good one!" Alonzo vanCleef called in encouragement. He was several yards away, dividing his attention between both Sydney and Sly. While the other two judges were in charge of the weigh station, he and Walker kept a physical presence among the anglers.

Sydney waved in reply, but his hand didn't make it very high. He stumbled toward the crossing, hoping his legs were steady enough to make it across the two boards that served as a footbridge. He kept a firm hold on his prize fish, guessing it to weigh at least five pounds. He made the assessment by its size. If he judged by how it *felt*, he carried a world-class record breaker.

Sweat dripped into his eyes, blurring his vision. That was the only explanation for what he thought he saw. Between the fever and the chills and the sweat running down his face, his eyes were blurred. He thought he saw an old cowboy dressed in chaps and a wide-brimmed sombrero, with a six-gun strapped to his side. But that was impossible. He shook his head, and the vision shifted. Now he thought it was that kid who worked at the inn, the one who helped him porter his kayak.

He stumbled forward, and his feet felt suddenly

156

wet, like they did that day at the river, with the water leaking into his boat. Sydney looked down, finding himself on the makeshift bridge. His feet were dry, but the rest of him was drenched in sweat.

He thought someone might have pushed him then. Or maybe it was the bridge, beckoning to him to lay down for a much-needed rest.

Either way, he went tumbling. His knees buckled beneath him, and he began falling, but he had the wherewithal to save his prized catch. Thrusting his arm forward, he flung the catfish onto the far side of the bank, preventing it from escaping back into the creek. The fish fell onto land, but Sydney wasn't so lucky.

He could have sworn he heard a sizzle as his fevered flesh splashed into the cool water below.

C

"Senorita! Senorita! Come pronto!"

Orlan's wispy form appeared before Hannah as she recorded Kent Haney's fifth fish of the day. So far, the man was in a dead heat with Rand. Sly hadn't brought any fish in to weigh, but that was to be expected in her condition.

"You must come!" the ghost insisted.

Hannah couldn't very well rush off in the middle of recording the official weights. Especially when no one could see or hear the frantic man before her. There was an urgency in his voice, however, that she knew not to ignore.

"What was that?" she said, sitting forward in her chair. She pretended to hear something. "It sounds like someone is in trouble!"

It gave her the excuse she needed to follow the ghost to the creek. Orlan slipped through the grasses and the leaves without a single care. He even floated straight into the gnarled bark of an ash tree and came out on the

157

other side, impatiently waving her forward. Hannah had to maneuver the rocky path and avoid walking into trees, but she wasn't far behind him.

She came upon the fish first. A nice-sized catfish floundering there on dry land, thrashing about like... well, like a fish out of water. It was large enough to give Kent a run for his money. Hannah considered picking the fish up, but a muffled sound drew her toward the water.

She saw Sydney then, bobbing there in South Grape Creek. His head stayed above water, but his chin quivered and dipped, occasionally collecting creek water in his drooling lower lip. He kept muttering the same phrases over and over. "My fish. Weigh my fish... Keep her from Tallia... Weigh my fish... Keep her away from Tallia..."

"Man down!" she yelled over her shoulder. "We need help here!"

Without giving it a second thought, Hannah slipped into the water alongside Sydney. It was shallow enough that, even with her feet touching bottom, her shoulders were above the waterline. Sydney's legs folded beneath him, too weak to be of any use, but there wasn't enough current in the lazy waters to carry him downstream.

"Sydney! What happened to you? You're burning up!"

"Hurt," he told her. "Hard to—Hard to breathe. But, my fish. Weigh my fish."

"Don't worry about your fish. We have to get you out of this water and to a hospital."

He gripped her arm with amazing strength. "Weigh my fish!" he demanded. His eyes were red and glazed with fever, lending him a wild look.

Just for a moment, Hannah felt a stab of fear. According to her highly unscientific question mark system, Sydney led the pack with questionable motives. Seeing his eyes ablaze this way, it was easy to imagine him as a would-be murderer.

Her fear was replaced by a rush of guilt. No matter what he may have done in the past few days, right now, the man was clearly very sick.

"Okay, Sydney," she promised, her tone soothing. "We'll weigh your fish."

"Don't patro—pat—" He couldn't find the word he was looking for. He settled for, "Don't tease me. You gotta weigh it in."

"I will, I promise."

"And k—keep her from Tallia." His chin quivered so badly she had trouble making out his next words. She thought he mentioned Sly, saying something about being tougher than she looked. For whatever reason, he seemed to think she might hurt the much larger redhead.

He sagged again in the water, still mumbling about his fish. His worry for Tallia confused Hannah, until she recalled the awkward moment the two women met along the trail. There had been no missing the scorn in Sly's face.

The bruise on Tallia's face was just now fading. To a suspecting eye, it was no longer visible beneath the many layers of makeup. Hannah, however, remembered the very distinct impression of a handprint upon her cheek. Had Sly been the one to inflict it, she wondered now. Was that why Sydney worried about Tallia's wellbeing? Perhaps the women had been arguing over him, and the disagreement had turned physical. Maybe he felt responsible, and the worry still nagged at his semi-conscious mind.

As people rushed to their aid, Sydney roused again, worrying about his fish. Hannah instructed someone to find and weigh his catfish. The others could help her get him from the water.

When she moved her hand's placement on his

back, he yelped in pain. A quick peek under his shirt revealed two places between his shoulder blades, both swollen and an angry red.

"I think he's been bitten by something!" she realized.

George Hernandez paused in midair as he was about to enter the creek beside her. "A snake?" he asked, nervously scanning the water. Sadly enough, he had already seen the effects of that.

"More likely a spider. And from the looks of these bites, it was several hours ago. He needs immediate care."

Several hands reached into the water and helped Sydney to the banks. As Hannah pulled herself up and out of the water, Kent Haney sent her a worried look.

"Are you calling the tournament?" he asked.

Hannah glanced down at her watch, hoping the manufacturer's claims of it being waterproof proved true. The eyewitnesses weren't here yet to make confirmation. She had to make a spur-of-the-moment decision. "No. There's only thirty-five minutes left. We'll see it through."

Without another word, Kent shimmied across the bridge and took off along the creekside at a run. He had more fish to catch.

# CHAPTER 20

    As they waited for the ambulance to arrive, Hannah radioed the judges that the contest was to continue. Calling the contest early wouldn't speed the ambulance's arrival, nor would it help Sydney's recovery. Allowing the tournament to continue would go a long way to soothe the fears of the spectators and give them something positive to focus on.

    Once the sheriff arrived, that could prove to be the only positive part of the day.

    As soon as the ambulance had Sydney stabilized and aboard, Hannah hurried to the inn to change out of her wet clothes. Just ten minutes in the hot Texas sun, and she was no longer soggy, but the wet jeans still chaffed, and her shoes squeaked when she walked. There was just enough time to change and get back at the creek for the official end of the tournament.

    *It can't end soon enough to suit me!* The thought ran through her mind as she hit the stairs running. The entire tournament had been one catastrophe after another. It was amazing they had managed to navigate the nightmare thus far without loss of life, but she knew they weren't out of the woods yet. Although he improved daily, Ahmed was still listed in critical condition. And it was entirely too soon to know Sydney's fate. All they could do was pray that everyone survived, and that the whole ordeal would soon be behind them. Hannah already doubted the odds of there being a twenty-fourth Trifishlon.

She peeled off her jeans and wet t-shirt, hurriedly dried off, and slipped into fresh clothes. She was back down the stairs and out the door in less than five minutes.

Hannah walked outside and into an argument.

"What did you *do*, Dawson?" Brianna demanded, poking a finger into the boy's chest. It resembled a deflated balloon, small and caved within itself.

"I... nothing!" the boy said, darting his eyes toward Hannah as she came out the door.

"I don't believe you! You had something to do with this!"

Hannah didn't have time for teenage drama. "We need you back at the creek," she told the two as she hurried past.

"Dawson has something to tell you, Miss Hannah," Brianna blurted out, much to her companion's horror.

Hannah held up a staying hand. "Whatever it is, it will have to wait. We have a tournament to wind up and winners to announce. You'll need to help with clean up. When all this is said and done, we can have a nice long chat." Already headed toward the creek, she turned back to add, "Meet me there in five!"

Brianna glared at the boy. "You heard the woman. It's time to clean up this mess you helped create."

Back creekside, Melvin Maddox and Bart Hinkle teamed up to complain about, in a nutshell, *everything*. The contest had been rigged. It had been one disaster after another. They demanded a do-over, beginning with the very first accident. Bart had researched the rules and by-laws, and didn't find any grounds for his dismissal, so he insisted on being included in said do-over. Melvin had done his own research and found out the Llano River was haunted. He claimed interference from ghosts wasn't a valid reason to be disqualified and demanded he be reinstated and given a fair shot at the grand prize.

Butch Tanger and Billy Joe Claus had tied for fifth place. They thought they should be allowed to step in and take Sydney's spot. They could start right now and be done by three o'clock.

"Enough!" Hannah shouted to the hagglers. "I have had enough, and I will not tolerate another word from any of you." Her tone was firm and allowed no room for argument. "The tournament is now over. There will be no do-over. Whatever decisions the judges make will be final. If you cannot stand there quietly and obey the rules, I must insist that you leave."

She stomped away from the stunned group with their mouths hanging agape. Sadie and Fred beamed at her no-nonsense handling of the troublemakers. Walker wore a proud smirk as he silently dared the men to defy her orders.

"This is basically a three-person contest now," Sadie mumbled as Sly, Rand, and Kent lined up for the last of the weigh-ins.

Hannah released a long, weary sigh. "Honestly, at this point, I don't care who wins. I just want this to be over with. I never dreamed a simple fishing tournament could turn into such an unmitigated disaster!"

"I must point out, nothing like this has ever happened in the past."

"Believe me, I'm well aware of that. *I* brought this on," Hannah lamented, "when I upped the ante and turned this into a free for all."

"You did no such thing!" Fred denied.

"Oh, honey, you can't possibly blame yourself for other people's greed and stupidity," Sadie said, folding the younger woman into an encouraging hug. "Sometimes, folks are just—"

"—evil," her sister supplied. "Mean and ornery, and hellbent on winning, no matter how much money is at stake."

Hannah sighed. "If Sydney was, in fact, the one staging all these 'accidents,' it hardly paid off for him. So, maybe evil didn't win in the end."

"Unless…"

Hannah looked at Fred sharply. "Unless what?"

"Unless he was actually a *victim* and not the perpetrator. I know most of the signs pointed to him, but what if someone planted spiders in his bed? What if this was just another attempt to narrow the competition field?"

"First and foremost," Hannah answered, turning to the woman in the Hawaiian print shirt, "Sadie, have the exterminator come out and spray for spiders. Just in case. Second, we need to stall this announcement. If Sydney didn't orchestrate all these accidents, then more than likely, one of those three people up there did. We can't just hand over ten thousand dollars, knowing he or she is guilty of attempted murder."

"We can't just put them off!" Fred hissed. "We've already delayed the tournament by a day. That crowd is antsy. And just look at the thunder in Rand Galloway's face. He's ready to have his name called and be done with this. I'm sure he's on his way to another tournament as soon as he leaves here."

"We have a small window of time," Hannah agreed, "between weigh-in and official tallies. If need be, we'll tell the judges to stall. It gives us a few extra minutes to think this through."

Sadie threw her hands up in exasperation. "What's

there to think through? We don't have any more proof today than we had yesterday. Yesterday, we didn't have enough to terminate the tournament and avoid a lawsuit, even if it was for the safety of our contestants."

"Yesterday, Sydney Branch was our prime suspect," Hannah reminded her. "He had motive and possible means and opportunity, assuming he enlisted the help of local friends and family. Being spider bitten doesn't mean he's innocent, but Fred has a valid point. It could be another of these uncanny 'accidents' at play." She nibbled her bottom lip before asking, "Maybe we missed something. What do you know about our other finalists?"

"Rand has been coming to the tournament the last several years," said Sadie, "but I still don't feel like I *know* him, if you know what I mean. He's a darn good fisherman, and he doesn't need to cheat, but I've been hearing stories this week that make me wonder."

"I know exactly what you mean," Hannah agreed. "I've heard the other anglers accuse him of playing dirty, but it's hard to know if it's fact, speculation, or just plain old jealousy."

"There was that business you overheard," Fred recalled, "about him playing with people's heads and hearts. I wonder what that meant?"

"I don't think I actually heard them call Rand's name," Hannah reminded her. "I just assumed that's who they meant, especially since I overheard the other argument, when someone else accused him of playing dirty."

"Maybe they meant he was playing around with Tallia," Sadie speculated. "Not only would he be messing with her heart, but it would surely mess with Kent's head and throw him off his game, knowing his wife was cheating on him."

"They also mentioned the pocketbook."

"If Kent lost because he was preoccupied with a cheating wife, it would definitely mess with his pocketbook," Sadie reasoned.

"So, we suspect Rand now?" Hannah ventured to ask.

Fred shrugged. "I think he definitely earns a question mark or two."

"What do we know about Sly and Kent?"

"It's the first time we've met Sly, so admittedly, we don't know much. But look at her, limping up to the scales. Surely you don't think she's faking her condition!"

"She's clearly injured," Sadie agreed. "Poor thing, she has to be exhausted, not to mention—"

"—in tremendous pain. If you ask me, it's high time a woman won this tournament!" Fred cried, unabashed in her favoritism for the lone female contestant.

Hannah made no comment, other than to ask, "And Kent Haney? How well do you know him?"

"Not well," Fred admitted. "I think he was here the year before last, but he was out after the first round. Honestly, I don't know much about him, but he's just the sort of fisherman we like to see come to this tournament. He's young, talented, low-key, polite, and—"

"—he minds his own business. Other than that wife of his," Sadie added, her mouth turning downward, "he's the model contestant."

Confusion crossed Hannah's face. "I got the impression you knew Tallia from previous years."

"Nope. We just know her type."

"So, we know nothing about our finalists. Any one of them could be capable of sabotaging this tournament," Hannah summed up.

"For ten grand, I think a lot of people are capable of sabotage."

"Miss Hannah. Miss Sadie."

Hearing her name called, Hannah turned to find Brianna behind her. The girl was clearly upset.

"What is it, Brianna?" She tried to keep the irritation out of her voice. She didn't need the interruption just now.

"I need to tell you something."

"Can't it wait?" Hannah no longer tried to hide her aggravation. "I'm sort of in the middle of something here."

Brianna shifted uncertainly on her feet. "I'm not sure it can wait, ma'am," she said in a timid voice. "You really need to know this. Now. Before—well, *before* you name the winner."

Something in the girl's pinched expression made Hannah rethink her impatient reply. There was a sigh in her voice as she said, "Very well, Brianna. What is it that can't wait?"

"It's—It's something Dawson did. And that I sort of did, too." The girl looked down at her laced fingers, worrying with her thumbs. "I, uh, sort of flirted with one of the contestants."

When Hannah would have brushed her confession aside as teenage drama they didn't need right now, Sadie patted her helper's arm and said in a comforting voice, "That's understandable, Brianna. You're young, and some of these men can be very charming when they choose to be. As long as that's all it was—" She broke off as a thought occurred to her. On a gasp, she asked, "That's all it was, right? None of the men tried to—"

"No, no. Nothing like that," Brianna hastily assured her. She darted a glance at Hannah before she addressed the more sympathetic older woman. "It was just innocent flirting. I knew he was too old for me. But Dawson... Dawson was jealous. There's nothing going on between us, but he wants there to be." She darted another nervous glance toward Hannah. "Day before yesterday, when you went to the Llano and Dawson helped with the kayaks, he—he admitted to tampering with one of the boats."

167

"Sly's boat?" Fred asked sharply, stepping up and into the conversation.

"No. He swears he had nothing to do with that."

"The only other kayak to sink was Melvin Maddox's. Surely, you weren't flirting with *him*!"

"Which one is he?"

"Big guy, balding, loudmouth. That one over there in the baggy shorts and high socks."

"Oh, God, no!" the girl said with a shudder. Her horrified denial was almost comical.

"Where is Dawson now?" Hannah wanted to know. "Why isn't he here telling us this?"

Again, Brianna twisted her hands as she dropped her eyes. "I tried to get him to come, but he's afraid. He knows you're going to fire him for this, but he's afraid you may press charges against him, too."

"Did tampering with the kayak alter the contest in any way?"

"No. He made the final four."

"Then I don't see why we would press charges. As for his job…"

Before Hannah could finish, the girl blurted out, "There's more! He did…He did something today. He's the reason Sydney fell into the water and almost drowned." By now, tears streamed down Brianna's face. "Please don't be too angry with him, Miss Hannah. Miss Sadie, you know he's a good boy. He just… He just made a bad decision. He didn't mean to drown him!"

Seeing the girl's obvious distress, Hannah softened her voice. "Sydney didn't come anywhere near drowning, Brianna. He has a terribly high fever, most likely from a spider bite."

"But—But Dawson said he pushed him. And that he fell, and that his head went under."

"That may be, but it wasn't under for long," Hannah assured her. "I was there with him. He wasn't

168

drowning."

Brianna cried now with relief. "He'll be so relieved. He felt so guilty! When he saw the cop car pull in,
he ran, afraid they had come for him."

Another thought occurred to Hannah. "Did Dawson have anything to do with putting the spider in
Sydney's bed?"

"Why would he do that?" the girl asked, her face
twisting in confusion.

"Obviously, for the same reason he sabotaged his
kayak. Jealousy," Sadie rationalized.

Brianna shook her head and said something that
sounded like a denial.

Hannah missed what she said. Her attention was
tuned in to Caroline, who suddenly appeared in all her
finery. "*She* was the one to put the spider down his shirt,"
the ghost said in her thick Southern drawl. Her blond
ringlets danced as she nodded her head in Brianna's direction.

"Brianna?" Hannah gasped.

The girl jerked her head up, surprised by the tone
of Hannah's voice. "Yes, ma'am?"

"Uhm...er..." Hannah faltered, wondering how to
get herself out of the current dilemma. Naturally, the
teenager couldn't see the ghost, nor hear her accusation.
"Uh, did *you* put the spider down his shirt?"

"Shirt? I thought you said... *Me*?" She was late to
pick up on the accusation. "No! Why would I do such a
thing? I abhor spiders! And I barely know the man."

"Wait." Hannah was clearly confused. She pushed
her fingers through her hair, trying to make sense of it all.
Surely Brianna more than *barely* knew Sydney, if Dawson were jealous enough to tamper with his kayak and
push him into the creek. And how could the girl sound so
sincere and look so utterly appalled, when Carolina had
been eyewitness to the deed?

169

Hannah looked to Caroline for confirmation. "You saw her?" she whispered.

"Not her," the ghostly image corrected. She lifted a dainty hand and made a motion with her folding fan. "Her."

Hannah followed her line of sight. All she saw was a frizzy head of red hair and a pair of long, shapely legs, but it was enough.

"*Tallia*?" Her voice was weak. "Tallia did this?"

Unaware of the other conversation taking place, Brianna looked more confused than ever. "How would I know?" she asked incredulously. "I have no idea what that woman does! But I've seen her with him often enough, so I guess it's possible." Her shrug was almost nonchalant. "Her father's seen them together, too."

"It's true," Caroline confirmed. "She spends a great deal of time with him. And with the man in the sleeping car."

"Sleeping car?" Hannah murmured. She had no idea what Caroline was talking about.

Hearing only her boss, Brianna repeated, "Sleeping car? Miss Hannah, are you feeling all right?"

"Uhm, yes. Yes, I'm fine."

In truth, she wasn't fine. She was thoroughly confused. Hannah tried to piece the facts all together, but nothing made sense.

Dawson was jealous of Sydney, yet Brianna claimed not to know him well, and she seemed unconcerned about his apparent relationship with Tallia.

It came as no surprise that Tallia was messing around with the fisherman, but why would she poison him? Had she discovered he was the one sabotaging the tournament? Was this her way of stopping him?

She had no idea what a sleeping car was.

And, who the heck was Tallia's father?

Realizing the teenage girl stared at her strangely,

Hannah said in distraction, "Thank you for coming forward, Brianna. You may go now."

"But, what about Dawson?" she wanted to know. "Are the cops going to arrest him?"

"No. They're here for another matter."

"I told him he had to return the money, at the very least."

She almost hated to ask. This tale was growing stranger by the moment. "What money?"

"The money Rand gave him to push Sydney in the water."

"*Rand* paid him to push Sydney in?" Fred gasped. She shook her head, as if to clear it. "Just to be straight. You're saying Dawson took money from *Rand Galloway*."

"Why would he do such a thing?" Sadie seconded her sister's surprise.

Brianna misunderstood the 'he' in question. "I know," she sighed. "First, Dawson messed with his kayak. Then he's taking money from him. I guess he thought if he couldn't best him, he would at least take his money."

"Wait. Wait, wait, wait." Hannah's head spun with the speed in which the story changed. "Why would Dawson mess with *Rand's* kayak?"

Brianna blushed and ducked her head. "I know he's way too old for me, but..."

Sadie's shocked gasp filled the air. "You've been flirting with *Rand*, not Sydney?"

"Please," the girl said, rolling her eyes. "Sydney only has eyes for Tallia, even though she's a married woman. And he may be older, but Rand is very charming. He understands me," the girl insisted. After a slight hesitation, she frowned. "At least, I thought he did. He's easy to talk to. That's all we ever did, by the way. It was never...well, you know. We were supposed to meet last night, but he never showed. I think he stood me up. I went to his RV, but he wasn't there, either."

"There!" Caroline said unexpectedly, causing Hannah to jump. She pointed her fan to someone carrying a hot dog and drink. "That gentleman received his food from the dining car. It's similar to the sleeping car where the man stays."

"Oh!" Hannah said in sudden understanding. "You mean the food truck. And the sleeping car is an RV."

Again, Brianna only heard Hannah's outburst. The teen eyed her boss warily. Inching closer to Sadie, she hissed, "Is she okay? I didn't say anything about a food truck. Why does she keep talking about a car going to sleep?"

Sadie patted the girl's arm, dismissing her concern with an airy explanation. "Oh, she's just the type who thinks better when she talks to herself. A lot of geniuses do that, you know. And our Hannah here is a brilliant woman. She's simply talking out a few problems."

Brianna looked unconvinced. "If you say so…"

"I do. Now, what were you saying about Rand?" Sadie deftly shifted the conversation away from Hannah's strange behavior. "He didn't meet you as planned?"

"No, he didn't," the girl sulked. "I sort of knew then that he had been using me."

"Did he ever ask you for details about the tournament?" Hannah wanted to know.

"Some. But, I swear, I never told him a thing. And then, when he didn't show…"

"He was probably off in the shadows, messing around with Tallia," Fred all but spat.

"Ew!" Brianna winced. "That would be sick!"

"I hate to point this out, but Tallia is closer to his age than you are." Hannah's voice was gentle but reproachful.

"But that would just be gross," the girl insisted. "She's his daughter!"

# CHAPTER 21

All three women stared at her, stunned in silence.

Fred was the first to find her voice. "Tallia is Rand's *daughter*?"

Brianna bobbed her head and explained. "His high school girlfriend got pregnant, but he never knew he had a kid until many years later. They haven't been re-acquainted for very long."

Hannah was still in shock. "You're certain that Tallia Haney is Rand Galloway's daughter." It was more of a statement, than a question.

Brianna lifted a stubborn chin. "Well, I didn't ask for a DNA sample, if that's what you mean. But that's what Rand told me, and I have no reason to doubt him."

*Other than the fact that he's a dirty rotten scoundrel!* Hannah's mind screamed.

"I guess that explains why he turned away when Tallia came in wearing that skimpy outfit," Sadie mused. "What father wants to see *that*?"

"Maybe the kind who convinces his own daughter to sleep with the opponent, just to mess with his head!" Hannah realized.

"And his heart, as the accusation went," Fred added.

"Does that mean he sabotaged the rest of the tournament?" Sadie wondered. "Did he try to kill the others?"

"Kill?" Brianna squeaked. "What are you talking about? He only told Dawson to mess with Sydney's fishing, not to kill him! Dawson blamed himself for pushing him too hard."

"Brianna, you'll have to excuse us," Hannah said suddenly. She steered the other girl away, dismissing her. "Thank you for coming forward. We'll take everything you said into consideration." She looked at her friends, crooking her head toward the weigh station. "Sadie? Fred? We have to tell Walker."

Walker wasn't happy about being dragged away from the official weigh-in.

"What is so important you had to interrupt? We're tallying the final numbers." His tone was almost angry, until another thought occurred. He craned his neck to see into the crowd. "Did the sheriff's witness ID our man? Who was it?"

"They just arrived, so we don't know yet. But we have something to tell you."

"You'd better hold onto your belt," Fred warned. "What we're about to tell you will knock your britches off!"

"This had better be good," Walker warned, thunderclouds returning to his blue eyes.

"It is. We think Rand Galloway is the one who sabotaged the tournament," Hannah announced without preamble.

"Rand?" he asked in disbelief. "No way. He's got this tournament in the bag. Why would he resort to attempted murder when he's one of the top fishermen in the state?"

"We don't know why," she admitted. "But hear us

out."

"We're not certain Rand sabotaged the entire tournament," Fred explained, "but we know he paid one of our helpers to sabotage Sydney's success fishing today. Dawson was the one to push him into the creek."

"That doesn't make any sense. Why would Rand—"

Sadie cut in before he could finish. "Probably because Sydney is his biggest threat." She hurried through the explanation, eager to get to the *big* announcement. "There's more! And this one is really juicy! Tell him, Hannah." She nudged the younger woman in the side.

"Apparently, Rand has recently reconnected with a daughter he fathered, unbeknownst to him, in high school. That daughter is none other than Tallia Haney."

Walker was appropriately shocked. His eyes rounded, and his mouth went slack. His hand came up to the back of his neck. "Wow," he murmured. "I never saw that coming."

"Neither did we," Fred nodded. "There's still more. Tell him about Caroline."

At this, Hannah cringed. "Yes, well, Caroline chose a very inopportune time to appear. And for once, she actually had something helpful to say. Unfortunately, hearing only my side of the exchange, one of my summer employees now thinks I'm certifiable."

"Oh, no, dear," Sadie assured her, patting Hannah's arm. "I think she believed that bit about you talking to yourself." She beamed up at Walker. "I told her it was a sign of genius."

Walker impatiently waited for them to make their point. His tone came out sharper than he intended. "And w*hat* did Caroline tell you?"

"Oh, right. She told me that Tallia was the one who put the spider down Sydney's shirt." She frowned then, realizing they were missing information. "She didn't say when, though. I'm not sure if it was this morning when she hugged him, or sometime yesterday."

"Judging from his symptoms, I would guess last night," Fred said. "I would venture to say it was a black widow spider."

"With that venom in him all night, no wonder the boy was so sick!" Sadie concurred.

"It's our theory that Rand and Tallia were working together to knock Sydney out of the competition."

"I suppose that makes sense," Walker murmured in agreement. He rubbed his neck as he thought aloud, "I remember that at the Llano, Sydney's kayak kept filling with water. Rand and Tallia may have sabotaged him then, as well."

"That wasn't them," Sadie said, making a face. "That would be Dawson."

"The same Dawson that pushed Sydney in the water? What's he got against this guy?"

"Nothing. He was actually targeting Rand. I have no idea how he got Sydney, instead."

"I do. As I recall, there were three green kayaks that day. Everyone but Sly had the same color. He must have gotten them mixed up," Walker realized. Then, "Why Rand?"

"He was jealous of Rand for flirting with Brianna."

"Flirting? He's old enough to be her father!"

"I know. But he *is* nice looking, and he can be rather charming when he tries," Hannah pointed out.

Walker looked at her sharply. "You, too?" he asked in disgust.

"What? No!" she denied. Her face was expressive. "I'm just saying I can sort of see how a girl could be charmed by a guy like him. Not me, but Brianna, obviously."

Seeing how Walker scrubbed at his neck, Hannah

knew something still bothered him. She didn't want to ask, but she had to.

"What is it?"

"It's just that… the guy is in first place. He's the winner. But how can we reward him, knowing he tampered with at least part of the outcome?"

"But he cheated! That's clearly against the rules," insisted Fred.

"What proof do we have?"

"Dawson says Rand paid him to waylay Sydney."

"Where is Dawson, by the way?"

The three women exchanged a timid look.

"He sort of ran off," Sadie admitted. "He saw the cop car and assumed they came for him. He ran."

"So, on top of taking a bribe, our star witness is on the lam. Not exactly a reliable source. Plus," Walker pointed out, "he's already proved he has it in for Rand. How do we know he's not framing him now?"

"Because Caroline said—" Hannah stopped without finishing the sentence, knowing the futility of such.

"Yeah, that one's not going to work out. We can't very well use a ghost as a witness." Walker's sigh was defeated.

"Maybe the sheriff's witness can identify Rand. *That* will be enough to disqualify him!"

Walker nodded. "Let me inform the other judges of what's going on. We'll stall as long as we can, but the award ceremony is supposed to start any minute."

"What a mess," Hannah grumbled.

"Try to find the sheriff," Walker said. He squeezed her arm to reassure her, but they knew there were no real assurances today.

"If I'm not mistaken, there comes one of our sponsors," Sadie said. "He's probably here to take part in the big presentation."

"Let's pretend we don't see him," Fred suggested.

"I'm not sure I can look any of them in the eye, knowing what we know."

Hannah made a valid argument as they studied the crowd before them. "It will be more embarrassing for all of us if we crown a winner and *then* find out he's guilty of attempted murder. I'd rather deal with the fallout now, than later."

"I see a uniform and a cowboy hat. I think that may be him," Sadie said. "Uhm, I mean her. Or, them."

Two uniformed deputies stepped from the crowd, bracketing a pair of young, scraggly men. Both looked as if they needed a good meal and a hot bath, though not necessarily in that order.

Hannah stepped forward to greet them. "Hello," she said, extending her hand. "I'm Hannah Duncan. I'm the owner of *The Spirits of Texas Inn* and the organizer for this tournament. These are my associates, Fredrika and Sadie Turner."

"Danny Arnold, ma'am," one of the deputies said, taking her hand. "Ladies." He dipped his hat in acknowledgment of the sisters.

"Tamara Ernst," the other deputy introduced herself. She jerked a thumb toward the handcuffed men between them. "These are the two responsible for rigging the river. They claim they were hired to do it but didn't catch the man's name. They say they can identify him if they see him."

"Right this way." Hannah led them toward the weigh-in station, speaking as she walked, "We have reason to believe the man who hired them is right up here, standing near the scales. If not, we may have to search the crowd."

The taller of the handcuffed men spoke up. "Nah, that ain't necessary. That's him up there."

"You're sure?" Tamara Ernst asked.

Her prisoner nodded, seeming to be offended that

she questioned him. "The dude gave me a hundred bucks," he said solemnly. "I'm sure."

"And you?" she asked his companion.

"Yep. That's him."

Hannah blew out a deep breath, dreading the next steps. Now they would have to arrest Rand Galloway, one of the circuit's most talented and revered fishermen. This would be big news in the fishing world, and it happened right here, at the Hannah Trifishlon. She wasn't certain she wanted such notoriety.

Stepping up on the makeshift platform, she caught Walker's eye and gave a barely discernible nod. She walked behind Rand Galloway and spoke in a low voice.

"Mr. Galloway, I'm afraid I need you to come with me, sir. Right now."

"Now?" he demanded, whirling around. "They're about to name the champion!"

"Yes, but I'm afraid there's an urgent matter that can't wait. Please, come with me."

"I'll do no such thing! This is outrageous."

"Please lower your voice, sir. I don't think you want to call attention to this." With a nod, she indicated the waiting deputies.

Rand glowered down at her, but he stormed toward the steps as requested.

Before Hannah made it to the second step, a timid voice called from the crowd. It sounded like it belonged to another young woman.

"Wait! I—I need to say something."

*Not again!* Hannah groaned inwardly. This day was a disaster. It was one surprise after another, and none of them good.

"You may congratulate the winners *after* the announcements, young lady," County Judge McNutt chided her. "Now, if you'll please wait until—"

"This can't wait," the girl insisted. The crowd

parted to allow her front and center.

"I'm not sure who—"

A middle-aged man stepped up to her side. There were enough similarities between them to tag him as her father. "I'm Lou Matejka, owner of *Luckenbach Poles*, and one of the sponsors of this tournament. This is my daughter Danika."

Judge McNutt's attitude made a complete turnabout. "Ah, one of our valued sponsors!" He also recognized the name as a generous donor to his re-election campaign. He was suddenly all smiles. "None of us would be standing up here today if it weren't for all of our fine, generous sponsors. We'll introduce them all to you in a moment, but let's go ahead and have a round of applause for them now!"

Without waiting for an invitation, Lou Matejka marched up on stage, hauling his daughter by the arm as if he feared her escape. Beside him, Danika turned a deep shade of red. Her eyes darted nervously about the stage, landing once before skittering away. She clearly wanted to be anywhere but here.

"My daughter has something she wants to tell you." Matejka looked past the flabbergasted McNutt and addressed Walker. "This won't wait."

"Very well," Walker said, making his voice as welcoming as possible. "What would you like to say, Danika?"

Despite looking mortified, the young woman lifted her chin and spoke in a clear, unmistakable voice. "I have reason to believe one of your contestants may have cheated."

A murmur moved across the stage and through the people standing closest to the stage, including Fred and Sadie. The sisters turned to one another in surprise, wondering what other revelations were in store for the day.

"How is that?" Walker asked.

"One of your finalists made frequent visits to our store this week. He didn't identify himself as a contestant. In fact, he led me to believe he was someone else entirely. And he..." She paused, having difficulty with the next part. "I—I may have inadvertently exposed sensitive information. I didn't mean to talk out of turn, but he—he tricked me into telling him details of the tournament." She dropped her eyes to her feet. "I'm sorry," she said. "I never meant to hurt anyone. I allowed him to sweet talk his way into the store and walk out knowing the secret locations."

Walker took in a deep, solemn breath. At least they knew who the leak was now. But what was it with Rand Galloway and young girls? Was he some sort of borderline pedophile?

"Thank you for coming forward, Danika. I know that took a great deal of courage and character to do so." He touched her on the shoulder and forced her to make eye contact. His blue eyes were filled with compassion as he smiled down at her.

He then turned to Rand, who had backed up to allow the newcomers onto the stage. "Mr. Galloway, do you have anything to say for yourself?"

"As a matter of fact, I do," he spat. "I'm calling my lawyer. This is the shoddiest tournament I have ever attended. If you think for one minute you can renege on awarding my prize..."

"You, sir, will not be awarded a prize," Walker informed him in a cold voice. "You cheated. And you very likely attempted to kill or maim at least three, possibly four, of your peers. I believe the deputies will escort you to your awaiting jail cell."

"They'll do no such thing! You have nothing on me! Nothing!"

Judge McNutt finally found his voice. "I think Miss Matejka begs to differ."

181

Danika shook her head and sputtered, "He—He's not the man I talked to. I don't even know him!"

Hannah's head swam. The more she heard, the less she knew. Today was a rollercoaster of insanity.

But she had to know. "If it wasn't Mr. Galloway, then who was it?"

"Him." Danika lifted her arm and pointed directly to Kent Haney.

Both men had the same thought, at the same time. They both dove for the edge of the stage, seeking escape. Standing closest to Kent, Walker anticipated his move. The agile attorney sailed off the stage immediately behind him, catching the fisherman by the ankle.

Rand made the mistake of diving off the front of the stage. Sadie thrust her leg out, causing him to stumble. Fred was tiny, but when she vaulted herself at the man, he went down like a ton of bricks. Together, the aging sisters incapacitated him long enough for the local Gillespie County deputies to cuff him. For good measure, Leroy roused from his nap and stood guard beside the sisters.

As a precaution, Walker had requested the deputies to be on scene for precisely this reason.

"Kent! Kent, baby, what are they doing to you?" Tallia cried from the crowd. She pushed and shoved her way to the stage, long legs flying over the uneven ground as she tried to scale the steps. Llano County Deputy Tamara Ernst stood in her way.

"Move out of my way! That's my sweetie up there!" Tallia fought against the other woman, trying to reach her husband. She was a tangle of arms and legs and clawing, scratching nails. "Turn him loose!"

"Stand down, or I'll arrest you, too," the deputy threatened.

"And you should," Hannah advised. "You should also ask her if she was the one to poison one of our contestants, via a spider. Most likely a black widow. The ambulance left with him less than an hour ago."

"It was all *his* fault!" Tallia screamed, thrusting an arm toward her father. He was now on his feet, hands cuffed behind him. "He put me up to it!"

"What are you saying, Tallia, honey?" Rand purred smoothly. "You don't mean that, baby girl."

"I do! I do mean it. All of this was your idea! You dragged me and my husband into your pathetic little scheme and promised to split the money with us. This is all *your* doing, Daddy Dearest!"

Tallia had never been a pretty crier. Hysteria was even a worse look for her. She pulled at her hair with desperate hands and made it stand on red, wiry ends. Black mascara and glittery silver shadow trekked down her cheeks and called attention to their asymmetry. Her open-mouth wailing was silhouetted in lopsided, bright-red lipstick. For once, no one cared what she did or didn't wear on her voluptuous body; no one could look away from her face. They all stared in horrified fascination.

"She's crazy," Rand said. "Her momma warned me not to take her in, but I have a soft spot for kids. But you can look at her and tell she's not right in the head. You can't believe a word she says."

By that time, Walker had Kent up and walking. They rounded the makeshift stage in time to hear Rand's accusation. Kent wretched free of Walker's hold and flung himself onto his father-in-law, once more knocking him to the ground.

"You sorry piece of humanity!" he screamed, shoving his fist into Rand's face. "How dare you say that about your own daughter! You don't deserve her!"

It took three men, but they finally pulled Kent away. Rand may have been handcuffed, but he was hardly defenseless. He twisted and turned, using his elbows and his legs to fight back against the much younger man. When they finally had the two men separated, Tallia managed to reach her husband's side. She all but dragged the smaller Deputy Ernst along with her.

Tallia and Kent cuddled together for as long as the officers allowed, kissing and crying and cooing silly words of love. Soon, both were cuffed and led away. As they traipsed across the field to the waiting cop cars, the Haneys and Rand hurled insults and accusations at one another, both sides blaming the other.

Walker quickly took control of the situation. He pulled a stunned Hannah with him to the podium, where he called the crowd to attention. Danika Matejka walked off in a daze, while Judge McNutt did his best to round up the tournament sponsors and salvage the event. Fred told a few jokes, and Sadie promised free refreshments at the inn when the festivities were over. Together, they rallied spirits and soon had the crowd cheering again. It was the most eventful and exciting tournament any of them had ever attended.

Perhaps because of the day's heat, or the day's traumatic events—or perhaps everyone was simply ready to have the event over and behind them—but Judge McNutt kept his normally long-winded speech to a minimum. He introduced each sponsor and thanked them for their generosity, and Fred encouraged the crowd to shop with them and support their businesses. And when it was time to name the official Grand Champion of the Hanna Trifishlon, Sly Patterson limped across the stage to a cheering crowd. Never mind that she was the only contestant on the stage; the sponsors and the audience gave her the respect due any champion, and she made a short but heartfelt acceptance speech.

As the first female to ever win the tournament, she also became the first-ever representative of *Luckenbach Poles*. Hannah wondered who was prouder: Sly or Fred.

Because Hannah had insisted on weighing his sole catch of the day, even in his absence, Sydney Branch was named First Runner-Up. His five-pound catfish won him one thousand dollars and a cooler full of beer and gear.

It was a wild finish to a wild tournament, but to Hannah, all that mattered was that it was over.

# CHAPTER 22

 One week later, Walker and Hannah sat in the fresh-air dining room of one of Fredericksburg's finest restaurants. Despite the late July date, they enjoyed a natural breeze enhanced by overhead ceiling fans and a nearby water fountain.

 For their first official date, Hannah had chosen a yellow sundress with flounces and off-shoulder styling. It was a much shorter, much trimmer, much more modern version of Caroline's billowing yellow gown, and was the perfect complement to Hannah's coloring. Her long, dark hair was swept into a messy bun with two long tendrils left to caress her cheeks. The sandals on her feet were white flats, the complete opposite to Tallia's four-inch preference.

 "Why haven't we done this before now?" Walker asked from across the table.

 Hannah waited for the server to pour their wine before she answered. "Maybe because you never asked me," she replied with a saucy smile.

 He accepted her gentle chiding with grace, lifting

his glass to touch against hers. "Note to self. Ask the beautiful Miss Duncan on at least one date, every single week."

Her laughter tinkled like the water behind them. "With our schedules, that might be a bit ambitious. Every other week, maybe?" she suggested.

"Done." He sealed the promise with another clink of their glasses.

Hannah turned her attention to the menu. "What's good here?"

"I haven't been here in forever, but as I recall, everything."

She perused the menu but stole a look at her handsome date. "It certainly looks amazing," she murmured.

In deference to the Texas heat, Walker wore a short-sleeved Western shirt with his starched jeans. The blue and white plaid looked good with his dark coloring and vivid blue eyes. Then again, Walker Jacoby looked good in anything. She had seen him in his tailor-made 'lawyer duds,' as Fred and Sadie called them, in jeans and form-fitting t-shirts, in fishing attire, and now in casual dressy comfort. It was difficult to say which was a better look for him.

Once they ordered, they enjoyed bite-sized chunks of bread, sips of wine, and each other's company. They kept their conversation off business and the inn, choosing, instead, to talk about themselves and things they liked and didn't like. They learned they had several things in common, but discovered they strongly disagreed on sports and movies.

"You're narrowing the field on our date night options, you know," Walker fake grumbled.

"I have faith in you. You'll think of something."

"Okay, okay. Let me think here." He pretended to give it great and serious thought. With a devilish light in his eyes, he snapped his fingers and announced, "I've got

187

it! How about… a monster truck rally?"

"Hardly!" She laughed at the image of herself at such an event.

"A tractor pull?"

"Same difference."

It became the theme of the evening. All through dinner, Walker threw out one crazy suggestion after another, only to be shot down by his jovial date. Reluctant to have the evening end, they decided to stroll along the sidewalk and window shop.

"I love all the old German architecture of the town," Hannah said. "The thick, stone walls and the gingerbread fretwork."

"It's a pretty little town, that's for certain," Walker agreed. "It has a rich history. I especially like the Sunday houses."

"Sunday houses?"

Walker tucked her hand into the crook of his arm as he explained. "When the settlers first came to the area, they claimed their homesteads in the outlying reaches. It took most of the day to travel to town by wagon, so many of them built small cottages they called Sunday houses. They came into town on Saturday, did their weekly or monthly shopping, and stayed the night so they could attend church the next morning. After church services and socializing, they traveled back to their farms. Most of the original houses are used as bed and breakfast places now. You'll find them all over town, dotting the neighborhoods with their fretwork or chinked walls."

Hannah stopped to read one of the many plaques lining the streets, mortared into the thick walls of the oldest buildings. "I like how these plaques tell the history of the town, and each particular building," she said, tracing the engraved words with a light touch. "It's nice."

"You should see these streets at Christmas. There's a big parade, and lights everywhere." Walker dipped his head in close as he painted a lovely picture for her with his words, using his free hand to pan the image in front of her. "We have a huge Christmas tree and this amazing German Christmas Pyramid in front of Vereins Kirche at Marktplatz. The whole thing is hand-carved and imported from Germany, and it turns like a carousel, with its nutcrackers and nativity scene and traditional Christmas figures. It's over twenty-five feet tall. The only one like it in the United States. And there's ice skating, caroling, and hot chocolate."

Hannah laughed, loving the excitement she heard in his voice. "When you talk about Christmas, you sound just like a kid."

"Everyone's a kid at Christmas," he told her with a confident air.

"Not me. Christmas is usually pretty low-key at the Duncan house."

"Your family doesn't go all out?" he asked in surprise.

"What family? My mom's in California, still trying to catch that next big break. JoeJoe tries to be stateside for the holidays, but sometimes he can't make it home. When he is, we do something fun, because that's just who he is. But when it's just me, I don't do much."

"That won't be the case this year," Walker predicted. "Your Christmas calendar will be chock full of get-togethers and parties, caroling and cookie exchanges, parades and lighting ceremonies."

"Oh it will, will it?" She hoped her voice didn't sound as hopeful to him as it did to her. To her ears, it sounded borderline desperate. She would love nothing more than to experience just the kind of Christmas he described.

"Yes, it will. And you know why?" A smile played around the edges of his mouth.

"Why?"

"Because I will personally see to it that you have a fun, full, and very merry Christmas." He lightly bopped the end of her nose with his finger.

"Careful," she warned. "I may just hold you to it."

"You do that." His smile was smug and utterly gorgeous. Hannah lay her head on his arm as they strolled leisurely along.

"Did I mention the mistletoe?" he asked. "Hey, that's it! We could go mistletoe chopping for a date." He picked up the game from earlier.

"Chopping, or shopping?"

"Chopping. It grows on trees, you know. We could go into the woods and cut our own."

"While that does sound slightly charming… no."

"How about to a mud wrestling event?"

"Definitely no!"

"Snowboarding?"

"In Texas?" she hooted. "In your dreams!"

"Moose hunting?"

"Again," she reminded him, her voice lilting. "Texas."

"I'm going to come up with the perfect date, you know. Something we'll both agree to."

"As long as it's not fishing. At least, not for a very, very long time. I'm still trying to erase last week from my brain's hard drive."

"I know the feeling." He moved his arm to comfortably rest across her shoulders. Her fingers came up to entwine with his.

"I still can't believe all of that happened."

"I can't believe the lengths they went to, making it happen. Especially when Rand was highly favored to win all along. Even Kent had been rising well in the rankings."

"According to George and a few of the others, it was because they had already pulled similar stunts in previous tournaments. No one realized she was his daughter, and they may not have inflicted harm the other times, but they definitely used the Tallia equation."

"The Tallia equation." Walker chuckled at her terminology. "I like that. Rather, I like the tag, not the deed," he clarified. "I think what they did was disgusting. They made Tallia flirt and flaunt herself in front of the other men, deliberating breaking their concentration. They used the distraction to their advantage, so they could win."

"Fred said it was a common enough practice in the rodeo, too. Perhaps any sport, but it still doesn't make it right. And while Sydney Branch claims nothing ever went too far, who knows about the other men she dallied with? I can't imagine Kent being okay with that, even if it wasn't anything more than a few hot and heavy kisses."

"Particularly when they claimed to be crazy in love with one another and only doing it for their future together."

"A future that will now be spent in prison," Hannah mused.

"I'm still stunned at how easily the Haneys and Rand turned on each other. Before they ever left the creek bank, they had inadvertently confessed to every sordid deed that plagued the tournament." Walker shook his head, amazed at such a huge legal blunder. "Kent claimed Rand was the one to set up the Guadalupe. He had a friend with 'home field advantage,' he called it. Rand accused Kent of coercing the locations from the Matejka girl. He lost no time pinning Sydney's poisoning on Tallia, but she turned around and pegged him as the one to buy the black widow spider in the first place."

"For Rand, this was all about fame. He was only interested in becoming the face of *Luckenbach Poles*. He was willing to give the ten grand to Kent and Tallia for helping him win."

"He didn't know Kent planned to win the championship for himself, just so Tallia could be on television and magazine covers."

"And to think, they would have gotten away with it, if it hadn't been for the teenage girls coming forward, and those thugs they hired in Llano."

"Don't forget Caroline," Hannah reminded him. "She played a part in this, too, you know. And Orlan. He saw Sydney go into the water and alerted me."

"You're right. I mustn't forget your 'special guests' at the inn." That was the term Wilhelmina Hannah used in her will when referring to the spirits.

"You know," Hannah confessed, "Uncle JoeJoe still doesn't know about them."

"Really?"

"It's not exactly something you tell someone over the phone. I'm waiting until I see him in person to tell him about the *spirit* part of the inn."

"Will he be able to see them, you think?"

"Maybe," she speculated, thinking about her uncle and his unique outlook on life. "He's like a big, overgrown kid, so probably he will," she decided. A mischievous grin crossed her face, and she laughed. "Maybe I *won't* tell him. Maybe I'll let him find out for himself. That may just serve him right for buying me a town, sight unseen, for my birthday!"

A mild look of concern crossed Walker's handsome face. "I don't know," he drawled. "I don't think it's turned out too badly, do you?" She never knew he held his breath, waiting for her reply.

"To be honest, it's turned out better than I could ever imagine." Her soft reply was rewarded with a squeeze of his hand. He leaned in to walk closer to her side.

"But," she added, grinning again, "I can't let him know that. Not yet, anyway. He still thinks I'm upset. He has no idea I'm the happiest I've ever been."

Walker stopped suddenly, a smile spreading across his face. "I've got it. I know the perfect date."

She looked skeptical, crooking her brow. "Dare I ask?"

"A day at the Guadalupe River. You said you wanted to go back. We'll spend the whole day there. We'll raft the river, maybe do a little wading, and then we'll have a picnic lunch. How does that sound?"

A huge smile spread across Hannah's face.

"That," she told him softly, squeezing his fingers, "sounds perfect."

## From the Author

I hope you've enjoyed this visit to Hannah, Texas. Join us again soon for more antics and action from Team Hannah and the Spirits of Texas.

Before you go, please take a moment to leave a quick review on Amazon, Goodreads, and/or BookBub. It may seem insignificant to you, but to an author, it means the world. Drop by for an e-visit anytime at beckiwillis.ccp@gmail.com, or check out my website, www.beckiwillis.com.

Thank you for reading!

# ABOUT THE AUTHOR

As an avid reader herself, Becki Willis likes to write about believable characters in believable situations. Many of her books stem from personal experiences. (No worries; she's never actually murdered anyone.) She's won several awards, but the real compliments come from her readers. Becki loves spending time with her family, unraveling a good mystery, traveling, dark chocolate, and strong coffee.

Made in the USA
Monee, IL
06 September 2021